THE BEAST OF BLACKBERRY LANE

by
Ray Cornell

illustrations & design
by
Anya Lauchlan

GOLDFISH BOOKS

Other books by Ray Cornell:
Gandy Lande
Thomas E. King and the Sky-Guider
Jocko's Talking Sandwich

Other books illustrated by Anya Lauchlan:
The Black Hen and Other Stories
Gandy Lande
Witness in The Pagan World
Ruslan I & II

GOLDFISH BOOKS
2 Grovehill Road
Redhill,
Surrey RH1 6PJ

http://www.goldfish_books@msn.com
e-mail: goldfish_books:@msn.com
Tel: 01737 766 477

First edition 1999

British Library CIP Data:
Cornell, Ray
Lauchlan, Anya (illustrator)
The Beast of Blackberry Lane
I. Title

ISBN 0 9535170 0 0 4

Printed in Great Britain by Redwood Books, London.

Contents

CHAPTER ONE

JAPANESE DREAD

A sleek, white shimmering bus purred along the countryside scenic route from Thaxted into an almost forgotten corner of Essex. It hissed to a halt on the small gravel lay-by that chopped a chunk out of the village green, in the half-a-horse hamlet of Cutters Bend. Twenty-three Japanese tourists grabbed their video recorders and Nikon cameras, ready to make a plastic image of everything interesting in the tiny village. The doors whirred open, causing a crash of hot desert wind to blast into the air conditioned coach, as if someone had opened the hatch to the Devil's bread oven. The pretty, blonde, Stansted Tours courier announced, in near perfect Japanese, that the tourists could spend precisely half an hour in Cutters Bend before heading off for lunch in Saffron Walden. The twenty three passengers ''Aahed!'', bowed, nodded, and trooped obediently off the cool bus. The September sunshine hit their sunhats like a red hot blacksmith's hammer. England had never known such a lengthy boiling summer. The courier gasped, trying hard to smile. She felt like a slowly melting Christmas candle.

One old Japanese gentleman remained seated near the back of the luxury coach.

''Had enough of this 'ere weather, have you mate?'' laughed the driver, as he tried to unstick his sweaty shirt from his sweaty back.

The Japanese man nodded politely, but he wasn't really listening. He was watching a group of four young kids at the far side of the green. The children were not getting ready to play some English game. He was an old soldier, and he recognised the look of savage determination on those young faces. Those four children were preparing to go into battle - a battle against some awful "beast".

The courier led her chattering visitors across the village green. It wasn't really a "green" anymore. A "brown" would have been a better name for it. The grass was dead and cornflake-crunchy, even beneath the shade of the ancient oak trees. She marched her gaggle of tourists towards the trees. She tried to answer all the polite questions, although she had to admit that she wasn't quite sure why the English in this part of East Anglia covered the roofs of their houses with dead corn - "It's called "thatch" actually, Sir!" - instead of the usual slates or tiles. She told the crowd that it was an old local tradition. The Japanese "Aahed!" politely. They knew all about tradition: Tea ceremonies - Karate - Geisha girls - Bonsai trees - Sumo wrestlers - all that sort of stuff - "Aah-so!"

Under the shade of the oak umbrellas sat a beautifully crafted wooden bench with "BOBBEE'S CHAIR" carved deeply into its decorated body. On the bench perched its maker, a six foot eight inch "giant" with muscles like an advert for a weightlifting club. The eighteen-year-old superhuman was whittling away at a walking stick with the razor edged blade of a gleaming knife. The tourists watched with their mouths wide open, their videos humming, and their Nikons clicking. The metre long chunk of hedgerow was being magically transformed by the young giant into the shape of a twirling, twisting snake's body complete with a hissing cobra's head. It wasn't just a walking stick. It was almost alive and ready to flick out its blood hungry tongue, it was a work of art.

The giant rammed the wicked blade back into its sheath and put the final touches to the snake's squirls with a sheet of sandpaper. He blew off the dust, smiled, and seemed to be satisfied with his creation. Suddenly he noticed the amazed Japanese audience. He jumped up onto his size fourteen trainers, leaping on the ornamental bench as briskly as a mad monkey. He raised the walking stick high in the sky, wielded it over his head, and screamed out a terrible war cry:

"Clear off eee stupid-funny-faces or Bobbee smash eee funny old faces in!"

The Japanese tourists took three hasty paces back from the raging monster while several of them shook so much that they dropped their expensive cameras. Only the pretty courier stood her ground.

"Stop showing off, Bobbee!" snapped the English guide. "Why do I always get this ridiculous performance every time that I bring some nice visitors to see you and your lovely sticks?"

"Shut eee face, old pointy nose," sulked Bobbee, sinking back down onto his bench and laying his club across his knees.

The courier turned and explained to the terrified party that, although Bobbee Lock shouted and ranted at friend and foe alike, he was, in fact, completely harmless and had never been known to even squash a flea between his fingers. She pointed out that when God made Bobbee Lock he had used all his best building materials on Bobbee's brawny body and had very little left to construct a brain with. The Japanese "Aahed!" with relief and stopped shaking. They were not worried about Bobbee being a tiny bit retarded. In the last three weeks they had come to the conclusion that at least half of the English race were "totally crackers".

"Excuse me, Sir," whispered a small man in a smart, lightweight, summer suit, "would it be possible for me to purchase your most fine snake-stick?"

"Shut eee funny old gob!" mumbled Bobbee, still sulking.

"How much must I pay for the snake-stick?" persisted the Japanese business executive.

Bobbee looked up with a wicked twinkle in his eye. He may have been a few trees short in his brain forest but, when it came to talking cash money matters, Bobbee was nobody's doom-brain.

"Cost eee ten pounds," grunted Bobbee.

"Excellent, Sir!" smiled the Japanese gent, giving a little bow while taking two scrunchy five pound notes from his wallet. Bobbee grabbed the cash, handed over the stick, ran across the green, and exploded into his rose covered cottage. He gave his mother the money and she gave him a kiss. She was very proud of her simple, but talented, son. Bobbee snatched an axe from the woodpile and dashed off down the road hunting, like a crazed hatchet maniac in search of another poor victim to hack into tattered blobs of flesh. Actually,

he was off to raid the hedgerows for another chunk of suitable walking stick timber.

The Japanese man admired his wonderful buy. He told everyone that it was an incredible bargain. He was quite correct. In the twee gift shops of Saffron Walden, Bobbee's famous walking sticks sold for at least fifty pounds each.

One young Japanese student wandered away from the main group around the bench. She looked worried. She WAS worried. Tomorrow her three week trip would end, and she would be back at Stansted Airport, boarding her British Airways flight for home. Her tummy fluttered at the thought, and she suddenly needed to go to the loo. She was terrified of flying. She had made seven flights in the last three years, because her doctor claimed that she had to face up to her phobia, but the terror still refused to go away. Every ride in the clouds seemed more scary than the first. A shiver made her body jiggle. She wondered how long it would take to walk home to Japan.

She strolled away to the far side of the green, trying to chase the screaming thoughts from her brain. She reached the group of four children. They looked up from the vital task of preparing their weapons of war. The student smiled and said: "Hello!" The children nodded a brief reply but said nothing as they returned their attention to the small armoury that was scattered around them on the grass. Their arsenal of "Beast-killers".

The student failed to notice the weapons. She was wondering why it was that while every Japanese child had black straight hair, these English, Essex-Suffolk border brats all looked completely different. Hair of red, brown, blonde, and tangled black curls. She had a silly picture in her head of four great armies meeting to do battle at this very spot, Roman, Celt, Saxon and Norman. She imagined that the armies might have stopped their marching, faced each other and said: "Listen lads! Why don't we pack in this stupid fighting and become farmers instead? The pay is much better!" She pictured them throwing down their swords and spears and living together as good friends and neighbours. She knew that all the history books would call her a liar, but it was fun to play games in your mind... She did not realise that when the Beast played games inside your brain, it was anything but fun!

From the corner of the scorched green there ambled a narrow, overgrown

country lane. At the entrance to the lane was one of Bobbee Lock's ornately carved signs.
The sign read:

> **BLACKBERRY LANE**
> **DANJER!**
> Wotch out eee Squidlers don't get eee

The student couldn't read much of the poorly spelt warning, so she ambled on. About fifty metres in front of her the weedy winding lane dived underneath a disused, moss coated bridge. On the far side of the crumbling arch was a tangled mass of bushes decorated with thousands of juicy black berries. The student recognised those supersweet bunches of nature's gobstoppers - What was the English name for them? - Probably something like ''Gooble-fruit'' or, maybe, ''Granny's delight''? The English would never give anything a name as obvious and simple as - Blackberries!

She dashed forward. Those berries were just what she needed to cool down her overcooked throat. She was a bit puzzled as to why no one had beaten her to first go at the mountains of luscious, lip-licking lovelies.

She was only a few steps from the bridge's gaping mouth when she felt a sudden evil chill cut a slice of ice through the burning air. The sun still beat down upon her head, but she quivered in the grip of a strange force from some invisible, snow-cool wind machine.

She stopped. She stood very still... As still as a rabbit trapped in the deadly fascination of a car's headlights...

And then she felt a ''something'' creep inside her head...

Bad feelings - Nervous! - Scared! - Finger chewing twinges of panic!

''BETTER TO GO! - BEST TO LEAVE!'' said the Beast, to himself, as he hid in the rotting base of the mouldy murky bushes.

The ''feeling'' in her head got stronger:

Evil! - Black as the Witch's heart! - Ice caverns beneath lakes of blood-red water! - Deep Devil eyes!

''ONLY A FOOL BREAKS MY 'RUN AWAY!' RULE!''

She was rooted with shock to the cooked, cracked ground.

Horror! - Terror! - F-E-A-R!

"RUN, BEFORE I SEND YOU A MOST DREADFUL DREAD!"

But her poor feet refused to obey her scrambled brain, and her trembling legs lacked the strength to flee.

"I WARNED YOU! - I ALWAYS WARN YOU STUPID HUMANS!" said the

Beast, to himself, as he flicked on the switch in his brain.

The gaping bridge turned into a large, rippling cinema screen. A picture appeared on the flickering screen accompanied by a full blast of Dolby Digital sound - A vision of the student herself - A premonition -

She was seated on a British Airways jet - She was petrified of flying, as she always was, but she was admiring the view of the soap sud clouds far below her window - and then - and then her seat burst into flames! Everybody panicked - She ran towards the flight deck with the fire chasing after her - She threw open the door to warn the pilot - The cockpit was empty, and the pilot was gone - He was floating by the windscreen on a yellow parachute - He waved goodbye as the flames licked around her shoes and the jet began to nose-dive out of control towards the rocks below - The engines howled in pain - The student shrieked, stamped on the groping flames, and jumped out of the cabin window - She had forgotten that she wasn't wearing a parachute -

The dream by the bridge switched off. The Japanese student screeched, sprinting from that awful place at top speed. Like a flying ferret she flew from the lane that led to visions from hell.

Back on the green, she flopped onto the grass. She gasped, sobbed, and tried to calm down. She told herself that she was being ridiculous. She MUST have been seeing things. She was so hung up on her flying phobia that she'd had some sort of - horrible daytime nightmare... Stupid! Riding in a plane was safer than crossing a busy street in Tokyo. Everyone knew that was true - but - the image had seemed so real - and the stink of sizzling skin, frying with fear, was still in her pretty nose. How on earth was she going to pluck up enough courage to climb aboard the steps of her homeward bound plane tomorrow? She jumped to her feet, shaking the memory of the "dread" away. She trotted back towards her countrymen, passing the small group of children who still squatted around their weapons.

"Beast got you, did it?" asked Jam, knowingly.

"Well, it won't get anyone else," snapped Rinty, "because we're gonna kill it dead!"

"Yeah!" nodded Calvin.

"Yes, we yopping well are!" agreed Yopper.

The student hurried back onto the luxury coach. She felt chilly with the ice of fright, and pulled on a thin cardigan. She chewed her nails as the other tourists joined her. They were cheerfully chatting and admiring the walking stick.

The big bus rolled off for lunch, followed by cream teas and a guided tour of Audley End Mansion. The blonde courier slumped in her seat and picked up the microphone. She felt like saying: "My shoes are bubbling with molten me! I pong worse than a farrier shoeing ten race horses at once, and next year I hope to get a nice cool job taking busloads of Japanese tourists to visit the North Pole!" But, of course, she didn't. She simply said: "Farewell to Cutters Bend and on to the picturesque market town of Saffron Walden!"

The old Japanese soldier took one last look at the four children's faces. He knew that look only too well. He knew just how they must be feeling. Years ago he had seen the same look on the faces of his mates in Burma, just before they charged the English enemy. Part excitement, part hatred, but mostly fear. The fear of going into battle against some awful unknown "beast" that they had never seen. A beast so awful in its power that you couldn't possibly imagine how ghastly it might look. Why would four young kids have a look like THAT on their clean, innocent faces?

Just outside Cutters Bend the coach slowed down to pass a large band of bustling policemen. Some were preparing dozens of "No Parking" signs, while others were threading long lines of red and white tape to the top of cones and stringing them around a field in the distance. Workmen in orange overalls were hammering in a sign which warned: "DANGER! BLASTING!"

The bus drove on as the traffic policeman waved his arm.

"We only just escaped in time," joked the driver.

"Why are they blowing that wheat field up, anyway?" asked the curious courier.

"Oh, it's all to do with them creepy circles in the corn," hissed the driver, in a horror film voice. "When that alien Spaceship lands again the field will be packed with billions of bombs - BANG! - Bits of hideous monster will be splattered all over Cutters Bend - SPLOOSH! - BOOM! - SQUELCH! - AAAHHHH!!"

"Idiot," grunted the guide. She was not in the mood for stupid jokes today.

"Maybe we should park here and let your Japanese customers see the great fireworks display when they blast the flints out of that old chalk pit?" giggled the driver.

"Yes," sighed the girl. "The Mansion IS lovely, but I've walked round it twenty times already this year. If I see one more enormous oil painting of the Earl of Suffolk, I shall scream and draw a pair of spectacles and a large moustache on it!"

They both laughed as the big bus whirred along the country lane.

In farmer Clugg's field the drill holes were loaded with charges of high explosive by Philbert Slick's workmen. Detonators were connected by long wires to a firing box that was well away from the danger zone. Philbert watched the work then winked at his brother Percival. Percival grinned a slimy, cooking oil, evil grin.

Inspector Braybrooke asked the growing crowd of nosy villagers to go back down to the safety of the road, "just in case of an accident while the charges are being put into place!" He promised that they could return to the top of the field in plenty of time to see the big bang...

Inspector Braybrooke had no idea that they would also be in plenty of time to see the Beast of Blackberry Lane.

CHAPTER TWO

YOPPER'S DREAD

Across the field from where the high explosive charges were being prepared, across the blackberry jungle, under the crumbling brick arch, along the narrow lane, and onto the village green, Rinty's band of warriors were making one last check on their arms and ammunition.

Jam had her school bag crammed with skewers, chisels, kitchen knives, hammers, and a shiny brass toasting fork.

"By the time you've decided what you're going to kill the Beast with he'll have eaten you and died of old age!" laughed Calvin, filling another small bottle full of Beast-roasting petrol.

"I still think that stinking stuff is too dangerous to use," said Rinty. "You'll set us all on fire if you're not careful!"

"Wimp!" grunted Calvin.

"Well, at least let me look after the big box of matches until you're ready to light the bombs," Rinty persisted.

"Oh! - OK," mumbled Cal, handing over the half full yellow box.

Rinty stuffed the matches into the pocket of her baggy, multi-coloured shorts. She still wasn't very happy about the deadly petrol bombs, but as Calvin had originally wanted to bring along his father's twelve-bore shotgun, she decided not to complain any more. After all, when you go hunting a powerful monster like the Beast, it wasn't much use arming yourself with a pea-shooter, was it? She stuffed her Granddad's Gurkha knife (a Kukri she thought he called it) into her backpack. The two foot long blade was as sharp as chipped flint, and Rinty was rather scared of the gruesome war machete. She also checked that her asthma inhaler was safe inside the bag. She usually kept it in her back pocket, but she didn't want to fall over and lose her vital medicine on this important mission. Thinking about the horrors ahead was making her chest tight already. She wiped away the long strands of red hair that were sticking to her freckled face, and watched little Yopper as he lashed a strong length of leather to his wrist and sorted out the most deadly stones from the grubby webbing pouch that hung from his belt.

"Bet you can't hit the sign, Yopper!" teased Jam.

Yopper sprang to his feet, loaded a large pebble into the pouch of the slingshot, whirled the leather strap around his curly head until the sucking wind sang out a screaming song, and - let fly. The stone "whooshed" through the shimmering air, missing the top of the wooden sign by no more than one millimetre.

"What a load of rubbish!" taunted Jam.

"Yop off!" snarled Yopper, as he whirled a second stone bullet towards the wooden target. This time the pebble smacked the sign in the centre of the "DANJER" word with a loud clank. Yopper grinned. Jam and Calvin applauded and cheered. Yopper bowed.

Rinty was glad to have the brave, little nine year old in her small army. Heck! Hadn't it been Yopper's idea to kill the Beast in the first place? Was it really only two weeks ago when she had witnessed the results of the Beast's attack on Yopper? Seeing that cheeky kid in such pain had given her the strength to plan the Beast's destruction.

Rinty had been sitting on Bobbee's bench at the time. The new school year had just begun, and already her class had been set some tricky German homework. It had been too stifling hot to work indoors, especially with mum brewing a curry for dinner, so Rinty's books and papers were spread out under the old oak trees. The homework was boring and difficult, and it was Rinty's fault that the work was such a dishwater drag.

Miss Paris had asked the class a simple question in German. She had also told the kids that the pronunciation, and the spelling, of EVERY child's answer would have to be memorised.

"Hast du haustiere? (Have you got any pets?)"

"Ja - er - ich habe - er - eine katze! (Yes - er - I have - er - a cat!)" spluttered Jam, with her finger scratching at her left ear.

"Ich habe einen hund und einen wellensittich! (I have a dog and a budgie)" replied superbrain Angela Wormwold.

Rinty's turn to answer soon arrived. She fumbled nervously with the Ventolin inhaler in her pocket. All this talk of foreign furry creatures was making her lungs seize up. She was allergic to furry and feathery animals. They gave her instant asthma, made her eyes itch and stream with tears, and caused her to sneeze the rooftops off quite a few houses.

"Ich habe - ," Rinty whispered.

"Ja?" niggled Miss Paris.

"Ich habe - er - oh, I don't know how to say it in German - I've only got some stick insects!"

The class roared down a rotten rain of laughter. Miss Paris switched off the giggles with the following sharp statement: "Amanda Wrint, the German for stick insects is Gespenstheuschrecken! - Have you ALL got that? - The WHOLE class will learn the words, and the correct spellings, for the names of the various pets in time for the next lesson. Perhaps THAT will stop you all from tittering?"

Stop them it did!

The whole class groaned as if they'd each eaten a tin of prunes for lunch.

"Why couldn't you say that you had a katze, or something easy, you straw-headed tonk?" hissed Jam. "You and your stupid Gespen - wotsists. I'll shove them up your left nostril when we get home!"

As usual, it was all Rinty's fault.

So, she sat on the bench and began to struggle with her German books. Suddenly, a front door slammed open, and Peter (Yopper) Pettit came flashing across the green. Tears were dripping from his nose, his eyes were red and wild, he was almost biting through his bottom lip, and he was struggling to strap his slingshot to his shaking wrist, and (Rinty noticed as a tiny iceberg rippled along her spine) his hands and mouth were stained with bright blackberry juice. Rinty grabbed Yopper Pettit in mid-flight and pinned him to the grass. It took almost a minute before Yopper gave up the struggle to free himself from the grip of the much larger girl.

"I'm gonna kill that yopping thing! - I AM!" he finally sobbed.

Rinty knew exactly what Yopper was talking about. She helped him up and led him to the bench, where he sat shaking and hunched. Rinty dried his eyes and placed a comforting twelve year old arm around the quivering shoulders.

"Mum didn't believe me," sniffed Yopper. "She just told me off for going down Blackberry Lane. Grown-ups don't care about the Beast!"

"They care alright," said Rinty. "They care because they've been terrified too, but they won't admit it. Tell me what happened, Yopper. I'll believe you. I remember when the Beast got me!"

Yopper told the story of his nightmare dread:

"I looked at those blackberries. Rinty, have you seen how enormous they are this year? It's all this yopping heat, my dad says. I sneaked back home and got mum's biggest pudding basin to carry them in. I know that mum is always telling me to stay away from the Lane, but she never told me why. It looks such a pretty place, not at all scary or dangerous. Anyway, I had to have some of those juicy jungle fruits. I HAD TO! It seems such a terrible waste to let them rot and die - I walked along the Lane and stopped by the bridge -

"HELLO, LITTLE CURLY-HAIRED BOY!"

- The bushes looked so fantastic - so sweet - so nice, and friendly, and warm - I walked through the bridge and -

"WELCOME, LITTLE BOY!"

- I pushed myself into the brambles and began to pick those scrummy berries. I filled the bowl in no time flat - I stuffed handfuls into my mouth - Crunchy! - Lip smacking! Gorgeous! - Oh, yum! -

"WHAT A NICE LITTLE BOY!"

- I began to feel a bit belly-bloated and sick - I'd eaten far too many - I'd been a real oinky slug - I wanted to go home -

"PLEASE STAY, LITTLE CURLY BOY!"

- It was dead weird - The bramble leaves seemed to be stroking my arms - I wasn't a bit scared - The leaves were soft and friendly, and their touch was feather light - Gentle as a floating dandelion seed - but I felt ill, and I still wanted to go home -

"STAY HERE WITH ME, LITTLE BOY!"

- The branches stopped being so gentle and started to scratch and clutch at my T-shirt - They tried to hold on to me with their sharp thorns - I pushed my way out of there - They ripped - They grabbed - They clung on to me, but I busted loose - I ran back to the bridge - I ran like mad -

"STOP, BOY! - OR YOU'LL BE SORRY!"

- I had almost escaped when I saw something awful - It was stretched right across the bridge's mouth - A giant web - Like a net of steel - An enormous spider - Teeth gnashing - Legs thrashing - Dripping poisonous acid all over the web and glaring at me with greedy eyes - It was horrible - HORRIBLE! -

"HELP ME, BOY! - DON'T LEAVE ME!"

- I hate spiders - I tried to scream, but no sound would come out of my mouth - The spider gnashed his jaws and crept towards me - I - I - I hurled the full bowl at that mammoth spider - I hit it right in the belly - It's crazy, I know, but the bowl went clean through the spider's body - It - It just vanished - Just like switching off a telly - It was gone - I belted through that bridge -

"PLEASE DON'T LEAVE ME!"

- I ran home - Mum said that I must have got sunstroke - She didn't believe a word of it - Oh, Rinty, I hate spiders worse than anything in the whole yopping world!"
Rinty soothed and cooed and cuddled.
"I AM going to kill the Beast, Rinty!"
"Yes," agreed Rinty. "We must kill it! Be patient for a while, and I'll get my friends to help us. We'll all kill it. It won't scare us any more!"
At exactly the same time that Yopper was being calmed down by Rinty, beyond the bridge, over the bushes, and way past the Beast that sent the dreads in your head, farmer Clugg sat on the padded seat of his expensive tractor ranting and raving about the terrible condition of his useless new field. When he had paid

out thousands of pounds for the small chunk of Essex, the field had been called "Nine Acres", but now farmer Clugg had given it a new name. He called the land "Old Baldy", and bald it almost was. Next to the masses of blackberry bushes, where new top soil had been spread over the filled-in chalk pit, nothing grew at all. Not so much as a sickly daisy. Halfway across the field a few, almost dead, ears of corn lay crying on the soil. The last quarter of the field had managed to grow a reasonable crop of wheat, but even this area was spoiled by a nasty rash of several peculiar circles in the corn, where the stalks seemed to have been spun around and flattened by some mysterious miniature whirlwind.

The man from the Ministry had told farmer Clugg not to cut the corn when it ripened back in August. He claimed that it might be unfit to eat and had taken samples off to Cambridge for testing in the laboratories.

So there sat the wheat, useless and flopping, and there sat farmer Clugg, cursing and grinding his stained false teeth: "Blast it!" They wouldn't let him harvest it, and they wouldn't let him plough it up and try a different sort of seed. They wouldn't even let him burn it. First it had to be checked and treblechecked... "Damnation!" ...Old Baldy was supposed to pay for his new Volvo car and his new combine harvester. Farmer Clugg kicked his tractor and cussed everything in sight. He was going to grab mister Percival Slick by the collars of his pinstriped suit and shake his bones, until the greasy little yuppie either gave him his money back or rattled apart into dozens of gory pieces.

Farmer Clugg roared over Old Baldy's bald head. A cloud of dust swam up into the sky and mingled with the farmer's filthy swearwords. The sweat dripped off his furious brow and sizzled as it splashed on the red hot tractor's sunburnt back and shoulders.

CHAPTER THREE

RINTY'S DREAD

"OK" said Calvin, jumping onto the soles of his scruffy old trainers. "Let's get the job done!"

The other soldiers followed Calvin's lead, and the small platoon of Beast-killers strode past the "DANJER!" sign, marching in single file down the mouth of the terrifying Blackberry Lane. Rinty felt a bit safer with the tall, blond boy leading the assault. He was only one year older than she was, but he seemed so much bigger and stronger. She was very glad that she'd plucked up the courage to ask Calvin to help her, several weeks before. She had asked for his aid on the day after she had made her promise to assist Yopper in his one-kid quest to kill the Beast.

She had looked across the high school, lunch break playground and spotted Cal, with his usual gang of teenage "cool dudes", leaning against the wire mesh fence that stopped the school children from breaking out of the playground, running amok, and gobbling up all the town's newborn babies. Rinty didn't really want to go near that ghastly gang. They were sure to tease her with their gum-chanking mouths, but SHE HAD NO CHOICE. She needed more muscle for her very important Beasthunt, somebody local who might understand the reasons for her fear and hatred. She bit her tongue, clutched the inhaler in her pocket for comfort, and stepped forward.

"Wotcha, Ginger," greeted Cal.

"Can I talk to you?" stammered Rinty.

''You ARE talking, ain't cha?'' grinned Calvin.

''I mean - in private,'' whispered Rinty, watching the other teenagers cautiously.

''Ho - Ho! You wanna watch out for sexy redheads in the second year who come to chat you up!'' laughed one of the fence propping gang.

''Spit it out, girl!'' snapped Calvin, becoming rather irritated and embarrassed.

''It's about - the thing in Blackberry Lane!'' yelped Rinty. ''I'll tell you about it on the bus home!''

Rinty scampered away from the laughter of the gang. She didn't care about those ''gel-heads'' taking the juice out of her. She had looked into Calvin's eyes. He wasn't laughing at all. He was scared. She knew from the look on his face that Cal had also met the vicious Beast, and she knew that he would listen to her problem, because it was HIS problem too.

He didn't listen on the bus home, because two of his mates were showing him pin-up pictures from Baywatch, but as soon as the clattering, yellow minicoach pulled up at Cutters Bend, he didn't trot over to his cottage as usual, he waited, and he listened. He stood on the green looking nervous and twitchy, while Rinty came straight to the point.

''I want to tell you what happened to me, ages ago, when I went to pick the berries in Blackberry Lane,'' she said.

''Yeah?'' nodded Calvin, looking very serious.

''I walked underneath the bridge,'' Rinty continued. ''It was rose blossom sweet, mossy and warm. I wasn't a bit scared. I couldn't understand why all the adults tell us kids to keep out of the Lane. I had a lovely glowing sort of feeling, like when you've been away on holiday and are really glad to get back to your own little room - your own bed - your own comics -

''HELLO, NICE LITTLE GIRL!''

- I started to pick the berries - I ate lots of them - They tasted like candy from Heaven - DEE-LISH-US! -

''WELCOME, LITTLE GIRL! PLEASE STAY!''

- I ate and ate until I nearly busted my jeans - And then I noticed that the brambles were waving - You'll think I was crazy, but the leaves were rustling when there wasn't a whisper of wind - The branches were beckoning me into the cluster of bushes - waving me into the welcoming jungle - I felt them touch my hair, and it gave me the creeps - I got the shakes -

"PLEASE STAY! - PLEASE HELP ME!"
- I wanted to leave - I tried to go but the brambles clutched and clung to my shirt - They began to cluster around me, trying to surround me - I was drowning in a sea of thorns - I tore myself free - I ran for the bridge -

"BETTER NOT LEAVE OR YOU'LL BE SORRY!"
- I was just about to run through the bridge when the ground just - well - disappeared - In front of my feet there was nothing but a giant hole that went down and down forever - I couldn't even see the bottom - I was trapped -

"I WARNED YOU! - STAY AND HELP ME!"
- I can't stand heights - I get really dizzy - Sometimes I faint - But I had to get out of that trap - I had to jump for it - I leaped out across that dreadful drop

- "NO! - STAY!"
- I couldn't jump far enough - I missed the other side of the pit - I slipped - I slithered - I grabbed at the grass and the roots, but they snapped - I fell - My feet were walking on empty air - Down - down - down! - And then I hit the bottom of that well to Hell - I screamed and stared at my body, but there was no blood, no bones sticking out, no pain - I wasn't hurt at all - The hole had magically healed, and I was safe by the bridge - I ran home - I ran as if the devil was setting a match to my backside - I never went down that Lane again - Never!"

Calvin grunted, as if he didn't believe a word of Rinty's story, but again his eyes showed his true feelings of understanding and fear. He sat on the brown grass, hugging his school bag to his chin while biting his lip. Rinty could tell that some sort of similar dread had tortured the teenager, but she didn't want to ask him what it was. She told Cal what had happened to Yopper. Calvin sniffed nervously.

"Maybe there's some sort of drug in the blackberries?" he mumbled. "Maybe they're not blackberries at all? Maybe we've been poisoning ourselves and

having an - hallucination?''

''You don't believe that,'' said Rinty. ''You know it's the Beast!''

For a long time Cal just sat and stared at nothing.

''It's obvious what's happening,'' he said. ''The Beast always shows us a picture of the things that we hate most in the world. You're terrified of heights, Yopper hates spiders and I - er - well - ''

Cal stopped talking and looked rather ashamed.

''I know,'' he said. ''Let's ask Jam Chivers if she got a - mind thing - in the Lane - Where is she anyway?''

''She's still at school,'' said Rinty. ''She's got cellos.''

''Nasty,'' grinned Cal. ''I hope it isn't catching!''

The two kids laughed - and that made the horror go away for a while.

''Yopper and I are going to kill that THING in the bushes that gives us all these loony visions,'' announced Rinty.

''What if it kills you first?'' said Cal.

They both stopped laughing, then walked slowly home.

As Calvin stepped into a splashing cold shower to wash away another day's coating of sticky school dust, a strange meeting was taking place on the far side of an Essex field known as ''Old Baldy''.

''Don't just sit there in your yuppified little car with your stupid googly mouth wide open. I don't want to see your tonsils. Get out here and have a butcher's at this wonderful field of best Essex wheat!'' growled farmer Clugg, to a small, greasy-haired man in a tailormade, pinstripe suit.

Percival Slick slid out of his Porsche and placed his shiny shoes, carefully, on the dusty dead soil.

''I DO see what you mean, mister Clugg,'' slimed the sheepish little man, ''I honestly DO sympathise, but I really DO believe that the lack of top quality corn is due to the severe drought conditions that the whole country has been suffering!''

''Severe drought - my corduroy britches!'' snarled the massive farmer. ''I suppose you want me to believe that the hole in the ozone layer is causing it to rain on one side of this darn field and not the other?''

''The problem may simply be poor drainage,'' started Percival, as the rest of

his sentence was choked off by a huge fist which gripped his silk tie, twisting it like a noose.

"Drainage? - Let's see how fast your brains drain out your lying head when I unscrew it!"

"I really DO think that the new top-soil over the chalk pit is - AAHH!"

"And I really DO think that you are a slithery, slime-balling toad. The problem is this - YOU are a conman! - You are a rip-off merchant! - You've sold me a field that ain't fit to grow weeds on. I've bought a field that's got a chalk pit full of - goodness knows what sort of rubbish, and the muck is creeping across the rest of the ground! - I WANT MY MONEY BACK! - And, if I don't get a full refund, I'm going to take that funny little car of yours and stuff it in a very unusual, and uncomfortable, garage, with my sharpest pitchfork!"

Mighty farmer Clugg rammed every word home with a hefty prod from his muscular index finger, until Percival Slick backed away so violently that he collided with the Porsche's bumper, slammed into the bonnet, and slid painfully to the ground.

Percival dusted down his expensive clothes and, hastily, dived into the safety of his car.

"I'll get back to you as soon as possible," he squeaked, as he drove away in a cloud of spinning dust.

"GRRRR!" snarled farmer Clugg, bending down and yanking out a handful of his pathetic dying corn.

"Perhaps I should try talking nicely to you," he said to the handful of wheat stalks. "That's supposed to make plants happy, isn't it? - OK. - Try this! - GROW, YOU PLONKING EXCUSE FOR A PLANT! - GROW! - YOUR MOTHER WAS A CACTUS! - YOUR FATHER WAS A PANSY! - AND YOU AIN'T TALL ENOUGH TO MAKE A DECENT BOWLING GREEN! - NOW - G-R-O-W!!"

CHAPTER FOUR

JAM'S DREAD

The four Beast-busters swished their way through the long grass and weeds that covered the track where no one else ever dared to walk. They were fast approaching the gaping green mouth of the waiting, tumbledown bridge. They were all silent. All four minds were taking a journey back to the day when they had faced their own personal dread and been almost brainwarped to death. They were not looking forward to the battle ahead, but they knew that they had to triumph in order to save a new crop of village youngsters from suffering a similar mind-clanging day of horror in years to come.

Yopper click-clacked the stone bullets in his pouch with twitchy, itchy fingers. Cal clutched a petrol bomb bottle and wished that he held something more powerful - a hand grenade or his father's twelve-bore shotgun. Jam had still not decided exactly which weapon to use and was rummaging around in her bag. Rinty drew the gleaming kukri from its leather sheath and watched it glitter like a mirror of death in the savage sunlight. She was gaining strength from the sight of the wicked blade, when a familiar voice boomed out from behind her.

''Hey, eee lotta clowns! - Get outa eee lane, eee old fuzzy-heads! - Can't eee read my sign? Eee Squidlers are gonna get eee and kill eee dead!'' yelled a booming bass voice from back on the green.

Rinty spun around to see the massive figure of Bobbee Lock waving furiously at them. In one hand he clutched a large axe and in the other a chunk of freshly cut hedgerow. Both were being flailed in the air as if they weighed no more than a couple of pencils.

"GET OUTA THERE, OLD WRINT!" the giant roared again.

"We're going to kill those Squidlers for you, Bobbee!" bawled Rinty.

"NO! NO!" screamed the superman. "Do what Bobbee say or Bobbee smash eee stupid old heads in. Get outa that lane, before eee get killed eee stupid self!"

Rinty stood her ground and slowly shook her head. She wanted to obey Bobbee. Like all the other villagers she had an enormous respect for the simple-minded young man, and not just because of his ability to make a work of art from a stump of tree, or because of her admiration for the carved signs of country life that told the name of many an East Anglian town. Bobbee may have been - well - a few pence short in his purse of brain sovereigns, but there were things that he knew which were of immense use to the whole community. Bobbee could forecast the following day's weather with far more accuracy than Michael Fish of the BBC. If farmer Clugg was planning some harvesting, he would buy Bobbee a pint in the pub and ask:

"What's the sky like tomorrow, boy?"

Bobbee would walk outside, sniff the air like a winetaster, and march back up to the bar. If the verdict was: "Fair to middling!", farmer Clugg would start cutting corn at dawn knowing that he was guaranteed a dry day. If the answer was: "Treacherous, boss!", Clugg would put the combines back in the barn and muck out the pigs instead, knowing that there was sure to be a downpour. Despite knowing nothing of greenhouse effects or global warming, Bobbee had predicted that this summer would be a "Burn eee brains off!" one, and Bobbee was never wrong.

Rinty also loved Bobbee because he was always so helpful to everyone. When the front wheel fell off her mountain bike, there was Bobbee to fix both the bent handlebars and her scraped knee. When she got stuck in an apple tree, there was Bobbee to climb up, pull her from the cracking branch, and climb back down with her beneath his brawny arm... You never needed to call for Bobbee's aid. Somehow he just seemed to know that his help was needed and, uncannily, there he always was... just like now. Rinty did not want to disobey.

In fact she was so scared of meeting the Beast that she was almost glad of an excuse to give up the attack... Almost, but not quite!

"I've got to get through the bridge, Bobbee!" called Rinty. "I've just got to!"

Bobbee cursed, then ran through the slashing grass to Rinty's side. He looked into her eyes and he understood how she felt.

"Eee be careful, old Wrint," worried the sad looking giant. "Eee ALL be careful, kids! - This ain't no hop, skip, and jumping muckabout! - This is gonna be bad - seriously bad! Bobbee can't come with eee because of the Squidlers, but Bobbee will wait right here. Eee get in a rough old fix and eee shout for Bobbee. Bobbee will run in the jungly brambles and get eee out - Squidlers, or no Squidlers!"

"Thanks, Bobbee," said Calvin. "But if we don't come out, I reckon you'd better dash off and tell our parents. OK?"

"Or get the yopping police and the fire brigade!" added Yopper.

The four warriors left their muscular friend standing in the knee high grass looking as though his small brain was being torn apart by confusion. He also appeared to know a lot more about the "Squidlers" than he was prepared to tell.

They reached the bridge and felt "The Feeling" -- the warm and welcoming breath of breeze. The Beastly bridge was holding wide its open arms to draw them into its lair.

"HELLO, LITTLE CHILDREN!" whispered the Beast, to himself, from beneath the rotting dead leaves of the blackberry bushes.

Jam had frozen into a chubby statue when "The Feeling" arrived to welcome her chunky body. Rinty gritted her teeth, squeezed the kukri's hilt, and held Jam's hand tightly.

"Come on, Chivers," soothed Rinty. "It's not THAT dark under the bridge. You can do it!"

Jam sucked in a lungful of hot air, screamed out a pretty good impression of a Mohican Red Indian war-cry to shake away her fear of the dark, charged underneath the bridge and out into the sunlight of the other side - into Beast territory.

"Come on, you lot!" she roared. "Piece of cake! - No worries!"

Rinty's chest was heaving and wheezing. She placed her inhaler between her lips and squeezed a blast of medicine into her windpipe. The asthma's vice-like grip was chased away.

Rinty, Cal, and Yopper ran beneath the mouldy, dripping roof of the broken bridge. Jam was already stuffing a handful of blackberries into her slurping mouth to calm her nerves and to stop her body from wobbling with terror. While Jam ate, and the gang tried to hide their fear, in farmer Clugg's field the last of the wires were being connected to the firing box and everything was being treble-checked. Inspector Braybrooke told the growing group of spectators that they could leave the roadside and come up to the taped-off area of the field in order to witness the big blast spectacular. The audience hurried forward to get a place at the front, where they hoped to get a superb view of the explosive exhibition.

Several weeks before the Beast hunt and the free fireworks display, Jam Chivers had accompanied Calvin and Rinty to a hiding place behind the school bike shed where she'd promised to chatter out the saga of her terrifying day when she met the Beast and had her own dreadful dread.

''Yes, it was just the same for me,'' jabbered Jam. ''I was only eight years old and my brain was fused for weeks! I walked into the bushes - all comfy, and cosy, and crumpets for tea, it was -

''HELLO! - MY GOODNESS! YOU ARE A FAT LITTLE GIRL!''
- All juicy, and sweet, and lip-smacking lovely - All bulging tummies and completely spoil your dinner -

''PLEASE, STAY WITH ME! - I'LL MAKE YOU EVEN FATTER!''
- I didn't see anything scary at first - Certainly no sign of some alien Beast - But soon the sun began to drop behind the bushes - I never did like the dark much - I always used to sleep with my bedroom light on - Still do, to be honest - Silly, I know! - Anyway, I thought that I'd best be cutting off home -

''DON'T GO, CHUNKY CHILD''!
- The bushes rustled and moved as if they wanted to snare me - They grabbed at my shoes like a man-trap - I scrambled back towards the bridge -

"YOU'LL BE SORRY, PORKY! - I'LL SEND YOU A DREAD!"
- I was almost out when something ghastly happened -

"I WARNED YOU, LARD LEGS!"
- A shadow zipped across the sky - There was a total eclipse of the sun - I
couldn't believe it - It got as dark as doomsday in a few seconds - I called for
my mum - I screamed and screamed and Oh! -

"PLEASE HELP ME!"
- The sunlight switched back on. I pelted fast for home. I told my mum and
dad what had happened. They just laughed and said that there hadn't been any
eclipse at all. They said that I must have been dreaming or suffering from an
overdose of Crunchy bars. I'd always assumed that mum and dad were right,
until you told me what happened to you, Rinty. Come to think about it, mum
looked almost as scared as me. I reckon she understood about the Beast!"
Jam sighed with relief, as the heavy weight of her dread was lifted from her
chest. Telling someone made it a little easier to endure the frightening memory
from her past.

"So, we've all had some sort of dreadful daydream, have we?" she chattered.
"What about our parents? My mum and dad just told me to keep out of
Blackberry Lane, they never said why."
"Maybe adults don't get attacked - we'll ask them tomorrow," said Rinty.
As the three friends went back into their classrooms, a local businessman was
leaving the town in an almighty rush.

Percival Slick left his pretty secretary in charge of his estate agents' office in
Saffron Walden's Market Square, climbed into his Porsche, and drove twenty
miles to the town of Drainford. He sped past the colourful sign that read
"ESSEX CHEMICHEM - THE OZONE FRIENDLY COMPANY", while
gazing in wonder at the weird landscape of bubbling tanks, gurgling pipes, and
steaming yellow chimneys. He rode up a multistorey office block in a musical
lift that hoped that he'd - "Have a nice day, Sir!" - and walked straight into
the office of Philbert Slick, the boss of Essex Chemichem, and Percival's baby
brother.

''Well, you idiot, what on earth are we going to do about this blasted mess?'' snapped Percival.

''Firstly, you are going to calm yourself down and suck on a good cigar,'' slimed Philbert. ''Then you are going to listen very carefully to me - As I see it, this is the situation. The chemicals that we dumped into that chalk pit are failing to soak through the chalk as they normally do. They are creeping their way back up to the surface and spreading across the field, am I right?''

''Brilliant!'' snarled Percival. ''One hundred per cent correct! Give that man a trip to Florida and a dinner date with Pamela Anderson! - You told me that the chalk basin would hold the poisonous liquid for a few weeks, then it would soak away leaving not a trace. It's already gurgling up to the surface like a geyser with a raging temper!''

''Listen, brother dear,'' sighed Philbert, who was used to his brother's fits of the panics. ''Your local council had already filled in eighteen other chalk pits in this area with household muck in the last ten years, and you've arranged for my - er - my waste material to be dumped beneath all of them, right? - All the other fields are flourishing and producing bumper crops, but in Cutters Bend the chalk must either have built up more pressure than usual or, maybe, the excavation had formed a natural well, catching the waste like a saucer and making it soak upwards. I've no idea why, but I'll sort the problem out. You've saved me a fortune in the last ten years, and now I'll help you to clear up this can of maggots... No problem!''

''There IS one big problem, dip-head! How are you going to scrape away all that poisoned soil without the people realising that it was US who put it there in the first place?''

''Tricky,'' sniffed Philbert Slick, lighting a large cigar and letting the clouds of smoke pour around his brain, until out of the mist came a simple but ingenious plan.

''Easy,'' he grinned. ''We'll blast the whole field with explosives!''

''You ARE barmy!'' growled Percival, with his frantic eyeballs popping. ''The flint and chalk will go everywhere. There'll be poison all over East Anglia!''

''That is the whole point,'' chuckled Philbert. ''BIG BANG! - Earth all over the place - Whoops, and a terrible tragedy! - How sad! - Surprise, surprise, the earth is poisoned! - Where can the contamination have come from? Answer: ''Goodness only knows!'' - Chalk pit blown to smitherydoodles! - Evidence completely destroyed - ENVIRONMENTAL DISASTER!.. But, all is not lost! - The heroes of Essex Chemichem will clean up the village and cart all the nasties away - THE WORLD IS SAVED! - Hurrah! - We might even get paid for our trouble, not to mention a medal from the Queen - We'll give that grumpy old farmer a few quid to stop his belly groaning, refill the pit with nice clean soil, dump the rubbish somewhere else, and everybody's happy! - Simple!''

Percival and Philbert shook hands and laughed.

''How am I going to convince farmer Clugg that his land should be blasted to bits?'' asked Percival.

''Your problem!'' laughed Philbert.

''I suppose it was the dripping pipes from your filthy tanker that made those crazy circles is the corn, was it?'' enquired Percival.

''Not guilty!'' said Philbert, looking puzzled. ''That IS a bit of a mystery, but it has nothing to do with me. When my waste chemical drips a drop it bubbles and hisses and burns holes through steel. A few drops would have dissolved the corn and would have probably sizzled a few stone off the gut of that slug of a farmer too. It's weird. The circles are NOT my doing, honestly!.. Probably kids mucking about!''

The two brothers shrugged, then began to rumble with ever increasing, evil laughter.

CHAPTER FIVE

BIKER'S DREAD

''Look at those yopping great berries!'' wowed Yopper. ''I'm going to get some of those!''

''Um-er-ummm!'' said Jam, with juice dripping from her chubby chin.

''NO! - Don't eat any berries, Yopper!'' ordered Rinty. ''Cal might be right. We all ate some blackberries before the dreads came to scare us before. Maybe it is something in the fruit that puts the horrors in our brains. Maybe they are like some sort of dope?''

''ERKKK!'' gasped Jam, spitting out a shower of pulp. ''What about me? I've eaten loads already. I don't want to get another dread! ... OH, NO!!''

''Calm down,'' said Cal. ''We'll soon find out if the berries are drugs or not. Jam's the only one of us who's eaten them, so we'll just wait a while and watch her. Tell us if you see any more eclipses of the sun, Jam.''

''AAAHHH! - It's not funny!'' wailed Jam.

Several minutes passed and, apart from the occasional rude rumble from her tummy, Jam seemed to be in perfect health.

''She's OK,'' said Rinty. ''It's nothing to do with the berries. Let's find the monster and kill it! Let's get it done with!''

Rinty pushed a pathway through the tangle of brambles... ''Whish! - Whoosh!'' ...the razor edge of her kukri blade began to hack at the bushes in search of its hated enemy. Jam heaved the bushes aside with her brass toasting fork and slashed at their base with a long sharp chisel. Yopper stood on guard just behind the others with a heavy stone in his slingshot, ready to pelt the Beast as soon as he attacked.

"WHAT ARE YOU DOING, LITTLE CHILDREN?" The Beast asked himself from the shelter of his hiding place.

Calvin lined up his three petrol bombs in a row and began to beat at the brambles with a wooden broom handle.
Fifteen minutes later, and the four brave soldiers had collapsed in a heap with trickles of sweat washing clean rivers through the dust that caked their faces.
"There's nothing here. Let's go. I'm getting hungry," moaned Jam.
"Trouble is that we don't know what we're looking for," gasped Cal. "These bushes are thick enough to hide anything from a mouse to an elephant."
The gang sat down to eat some blackberry refreshment and to have a good hard think.

"THAT'S IT! - EAT MY LOVELY BERRIES - AND STAY!"

"Maybe the yopping Beast doesn't send out dreads any more," suggested Yopper.
"Well, it certainly gave that Japanese lady a scare a while ago. Did you see her face? She was petrified!" said Rinty.
The kids were tired and puzzled. They felt as if they had put their heads in a lion's mouth and were waiting for the jaws to slam shut. They already knew that the Beast sent adults a mind-mulching vision whenever a grown-up approached the bridge, whereas the Beast always seemed to allow any child through the bridge before scaring the pants off them. They had found out this information after asking some clever questions a few weeks before...

It was on the Saturday following the secret meeting behind the bike shed at school. Everyone had been given some research to do. Rinty wanted to make a really good plan before she faced the Beast in his dark delicious den.
Jam was sent to the library in Saffron Walden. She told the Librarian that she was doing a class project on the village of Cutters Bend. The patient lady produced a mountain of manuscripts, newspapers and old maps. Jam waded through the large heap of history all morning. Basically, she found out that

nothing of any importance had ever happened in Cutters Bend (she already knew that!) except for something very strange that occurred in the year 1872...

The London-East Anglian Railway had been building a single track, branch line from Thaxted to Cambridge. The work was progressing well on time until the metal rails reached Cutters Bend. A brick bridge had to be built to carry the trains across the shallow valley. The bridge had never been finished. There were dozens of reports of workmen going mad, seeing monsters and maniacs, ghosts and goblins, witches and werewolves, and having all manner of daylight nightmares. In the end not one single man would work on the bridge. A year later the whole scheme had been abandoned.

"Of course! - I've cracked it!" thought Jam. "There was only one old bridge in Cutter's Bend - the Beast's bridge! So, people had been getting crazy dreads in that awful place for over a hundred years. Maybe the workers had dug up some alien space capsule? - No wonder the grown-ups were so chicken-shaking scared of the place and didn't want to talk about it!"
Jam dashed home from her research to report to Rinty.

Calvin tried to chat to the adults in the village. Unfortunately, very few of them were willing to say much more than:
"You'll keep away from that Lane if you know what's what!" Or:
"That old bridge will collapse and crush the guts out of ya!" -"There's a lot of things that you young plonks don't understand!" etc.
The only adult who admitted to seeing anything unusual by the bridge had been old Porter Carter. Porter puffed on his bubbling pipe and rambled on about being chased by a fifty metre long python when he was just a little sproglet.
"Why don't you adults tell the police about the visions in the Lane?" asked Calvin.
"Oh, right, my beauty," chortled the wrinkled villager. "And what are they young coppers going to say about a bloke what reports being eaten alive seventy years ago by a monster snake what wasn't really there? They'd say I was crackers, wouldn't they, boy? I ain't ready to be sent to the nut-house yet awhile, but I'll tell thee something - It happened! - It happened right and true, and it scared my breakfast, dinner, and tea, right out of my belly! - That it did!"

Rinty had decided to talk to Bobbee Lock. She figured that, maybe, walking a touch on the simple side of the street, he wouldn't be so scared to give her some hard facts about the Beast - he wasn't!

"Eee go down eee old Lane and eee Squidlers get eee for sure!" said Bobbee, as he sat slashing away at yet another walking stick.

"Yes, Bobbee," smiled Rinty. "But what EXACTLY are The Squidlers? I mean, what do they actually look like?"

"Eee Squidlers look like eee Squidlers, stupid-head Amanda Wrint!" Bobbee grunted, as if he were talking to an absolute idiot who didn't know socks from sunshine. "When Bobbee was a little sprog, mummy say: "Bobbee, be a good boy or eee Squidlers will climb down eee old chimney and bite eee fat nose of eee fat face... Mummy shout: "Bobbee, stop carving those pictures on my kitchen chair legs or eee Squidlers will tan eee fat backside for eee!" - Mummy say: -

Rinty left Bobbee chattering about his toddler days, as she was beginning to realise the truth - There was no such thing as a "Squidler" - It was just a silly word that Bobbee's mum had used to frighten him with when he was being naughty - a bit like a "bogey man" who might "come and get ya if you're bad!" Bobbee didn't just believe that there were Squidlers in the Lane, apparently he imagined that they were everywhere. Maybe he had always obeyed his mother and kept well away from the bridge. Was it possible that Bobbee Lock was the only person in the village who had never attempted to eat those sinister blackberries?

Yopper saw his seventeen year old brother, Patrick, on the green with two other leather legged bikers and wondered if it might be a good idea to ask if the Beast would allow teenagers through the screen of his television bridge.

"What do you want, you foul-mouthed little squirt?" mumbled Patrick, as his younger brother trotted over.

"I bet you yopping punks couldn't ride those rust-heap bikes across the fields like real dirt-trackers do," challenged Yopper.

"Slug off and snog your hamster, brat!" growled Patrick.

"Of course we could," said biker number one.

"Give me a ride down Blackberry Lane, then," grinned Yopper, as the six-footer took the bait.

Patrick's face went as white as Persil.

"We can't," he replied, softly. "You haven't got a helmet"

"Don't need to wear a helmet if I'm not on the yopping road," grinned Yopper.

"You smart-gobbed little snot-sucker," cursed Patrick, as his left eye began to twitch with terror. "I'm not riding down that filthy lane. I've just spent all morning polishing this bike!"

The other bikers looked amazed at Patrick's lack of bravado.

"I'll give you a ride down the lane, kid," said biker number one. "Get on the back."

Yopper climbed onto the blue Norton and clung on tight to the chains of the biker's denim jacket. Patrick looked terrified, but he wasn't going to say another word in front of his "well hard" mates from Thaxted.

The biker kick-started the Norton, and it growled into life with a burst of smoke from the mouth of its chrome-plated, twin exhaust pipes.

The bike bounced over the grass-hidden ruts, and Yopper bounced on top of it. The biker was moving quite carefully, partly because of the Lane's rugged, invisible surface, but mostly because he was really rather a sensible lad who didn't want his cheeky pillion passenger to fall off and break something vital - like his tongue.

"Do you want to go through that bridge, kid?" the biker yelled over his shoulder.

"Yeah!" screamed Yopper, who was having such a fantastic time that he'd forgotten about the Beast - almost.

A few metres from the bridge, the biker felt a shivering shiver of icy fear that cut clean through his padded helmet and stabbed into his brain -

Creepy! - Chattering teeth! - Bat Out Of Hell with jaws dripping death!

"BETTER NOT COME ANY CLOSER!"

- The flash of fright took a firm grip on the biker's body, causing him to stiffen in the saddle -

"BETTER LEAVE - OR ELSE!"

The biker snapped off the throttle's roar. He jammed on the brakes and stared through his visor at the Technicolor screen which was showing a movie directed by the Beast - He was astonished to see a vivid picture of himself come flickering onto the brick cinema -

- He was burning up the motorway on his beloved Norton motorbike - The speedometer was touching one hundred and ten miles per hour - The wind was howling past the biker's helmet while the machine's powerful engine screamed even louder - And then the biker also started to scream - Something was mindbogglingly wrong - He was thundering along on the wrong side of the road! - A charging line of cars and vans were rolling straight at him - Their snarling radiators were snapping like the mouths of metal fanged monsters, their headlights were blazing, fire-red eyes, their exhausts were fuming foul smoke from a dirty dragon's fangs, and they were going to squash him flatter than a blob of steamrollered chewing gum - He dodged to the right side of a red Cavalier, left around a black Rover, jumped clean over the roof of an MG sports car - One second he was riding on the hard shoulder and the next he was bouncing off the central steel crash barrier - He threw the whining bike from side to side in a frantic attempt to save himself from extinction - He braked, but nothing would slow his wild gallop - And then he saw it! - It was heading straight for him - The biggest truck that he had ever seen - It filled all three lanes of the motorway and spread from the grassy bank to the barrier - There was no place left to hide - Nowhere to ride - He saw the awful face of the ghostly driver as he hit the truck's enormous bumper - The spectral driver grinned a deathly grin of satisfaction -

In real life, the biker woke up in Addenbrooke's Hospital with a badly bruised leg and most of the skin scraped off his arm. He wasn't seriously injured and was allowed to go home the same day. He'd always had a sort of dread that one day he would crash that stupid bike. He couldn't even remember his collision with the bridge, but he would never forget bouncing off the bumper of the nightmare truck.

Three days later he sold his scuffed machine and bought himself a sweet little red Metro. He named his car Gertie and was much more relaxed in the comfortable seat, with the safe metal shell to protect him.

Yopper, who had been clinging to the pillion seat, knew nothing of the biker's dread. To him, the bridge had been as warm and welcoming as ever. He couldn't understand why his brother's friend had suddenly braked, screamed, and smashed the shining Norton into the wall at the entrance to the bridge. Yopper was very relieved that the biker had been travelling so slowly and that he had the soft pillow of the teenager's back to cushion him from the crash. Yopper wasn't hurt at all. At least he wasn't hurt until his father gave him, and his brother Patrick, a smack round the ear for being ''a couple of disobedient nerd-brains with no more common sense than a lump of earwax!''.

After tea on that fateful Saturday, seven days before their attack on the Beast's stronghold, the four Beast-hunters had met on the green to compare the notes from their various surveys. Rinty decided that they should go around to the other side of the bridge. She wanted to find out if it was possible to reach the bridge from the field side. Looking from Old Baldy's edge, the blackberry bushes seemed to go forever and the briars were so high that the Beast's bridge was hidden from the kids in the field. The bushes were more like a blackberry forest, and there was no lane cutting a path into their horrid heart.

Jam looked around her feet and wondered why nothing was growing where the old chalk pit had been. The others shrugged.
Yopper wondered why the corn on the far side of the field had ''yopping great circles in it, as if the Beast had been stomping around on his king-size claws?'' The gang shrugged again.

All four crushed a pathway a few metres into the brambles before giving up and sitting down to pull the slivers and thorns from their prickled arms and legs. Rinty sighed. They seemed to be getting nowhere very quickly. The puzzle was like a maze - the nearer you got to the centre, the more you were totally lost... What had she learned so far? ...Adults, and teenage bikers, were not allowed beneath the bridge, and yet children were warmly welcomed into the Beast's den and were then scared to death! - Why not give EVERYONE the dreads in the same place?
''Maybe the Beast only likes eating kids?'' suggested Yopper. ''Adults might be too tough for his false teeth to chomp?''

"Yop off, germ-breath!" gasped Jam, hoping that Yopper's theory wasn't correct.

- And the Beast had been terrifying people in Cutters Bend for years. Or at least as far back as 1872. Maybe the bridge builders had done something to make the Beast really furious? - Maybe they'd disturbed a Red Indian burial ground like the people in Poltergeist? - "Jeepers in a jumper! This was one for Sherlock Holmes and no mistake!"

"What was that noise?" Yopper suddenly hissed, crouching lower in the brambles.

Jam heard the roaring sound and began to shake all over - and there was a lot of Jam to shake.

Cal peeped out from the shelter of the bushes as the sound grew louder.

"It's a car!" he whispered. " And a tractor! - OH, NO! - It's farmer Clugg! - If he catches us in his field we'll be chopped and mulched into pig's swill! - Stay down! - Hide!"

They hid, and they watched, and they listened with jingling nerves.

The shiny black Porsche and the dusty yellow tractor met nose to nose on the dead dirt right in front of four pairs of small petrified eyes and four pairs of small, straining ears.

"Blow it up with dynamite?!" roared farmer Clugg. "You're barmy - I've got a much better idea: why don't we drop an atom bomb on Old Baldy? Then I can drive down the hole, in this here tractor, and start up a sheep farm in Australia?"

Percival Slick giggled, weakly.

"The thing is, mister Clugg," he continued, "my brother is one of the Country's top chemical engineers. He has made many tests on samples of your poor quality soil and the problem is quite clear. The waste material that the Council used to fill in the chalk pit has been packed much too tightly - too many heavy plants crossing, as they say. The roots of the crops cannot breathe. The water table cannot rise far enough to moisten the top soil at the surface. Naturally, the plants have died from lack of sustenance. The explosive solution that we propose will loosen the soil, allow the water to rise to the correct level, and thus revitalise the land."

Farmer Clugg was speechless - A very rare state for him to be in! He had a suspicious feeling deep down beneath the wide leather belt that held up his wide leather belly, that the slippery, young greaseball was lying his snout off, but, well, it all sounded quite sensible, didn't it? Anyway - it wasn't costing him a penny piece, and Slick had promised him some cash to compensate for the loss of this year's ruined crop.

"Couldn't I just plough it up?" he asked at last, still feeling rather bewildered.

"It wouldn't have the same desired effect. The problem lies deep in the bowels of the earth. We've simply GOT to shake up the whole in-fill area!" slimed Slick.

"And what about those circles in my good wheat? How do you explain that, master Brain of Britain?"

"Natural phenomena," said Percival. "Lots of others in the West Country! Saw them on television! The hole in the ozone layer is causing the air currents to spiral in a tighter formation, while the greenhouse effect causes ripples in the cloud structure - thus producing a miniature whirlwind in certain areas!"

Farmer Clugg looked as if he didn't understand a word - which he didn't! He gave up the argument, grunted, scratched his rugged chin, and clambered back onto the seat of his tractor - He felt a bit deflated.

"It had better work or else I'll stick a stick of dynamite up your exhaust pipe!" he finally grunted.

"Oh, it will! It will!" sweetly smiled Percival Slick.

The four children wriggled out from their hiding hole as the machines revved away. "This is like some bad dream!" groaned Jam. "It's even worse than when the school canteen runs out of Chelsea buns! The Beast will be well choked if they blow his tail off! - Idiots!"

Jam, Cal, and Rinty went home to watch Casualty, while Yopper got sent to bed early for being the world's smallest Hell's Angel and almost having to be sent to Casualty.

CHAPTER SIX

MULTIPLE DREADS

The four Beast-hunters sat eating blackberries and wondering what to do next.

"THAT'S RIGHT, LITTLE CHILDREN! - STAY WITH ME!"

"There's only one thing for it," said Calvin. "We'll torch the whole lot! I'll chuck my petrol bombs in. Rinty, you've got the matches, light this old rag and hurl it into the bushes when I give the word. As soon as the fire starts we'll all run back to the bridge. The fire won't come through the tunnel because there's nothing to burn. If the Beast tries to escape a frying we'll hack it to death - and if he doesn't he'll be toasted alive! - Got it!"

"YOU'D BETTER NOT TRY IT, CHILDREN!"

"I don't like it," said Rinty, shaking her dusty red head. "It's too dangerous, and we'll get slaughtered by our parents when they see the fire from the other side of the bushes. The whole village is over there watching the explosion. They'll see the smoke and we'll get hell and high tide for it!"
"Their explosion will hide the flames! - It's perfect!" said Cal.
"Another thing," said Jam. "It's just not fair to burn something... It's fighting dirty!"
"Dirty?" gasped Calvin. "I suppose that scaring a whole village with crazy visions is your idea of a fair fight? Why don't you go and get a referee for the match and we'll all suck a lemon at half time, you lard-limbed wimp?"

"We still don't know why the Beast sends the visions, Yopper whispered, shyly. "For all we know he might be more scared of us than we are of him."
Calvin was furious. "This was YOUR idea, you little pain! Well, you lot can chicken out if you want to, but I'm going to kill that Beast!" he yelled.
Cal snatched the matches from Rinty and started to hack a fresh path into the heart of the bushes. The others watched nervously as he began to unscrew the top of his first petrol bomb.

"YOU ARE A MENACE, YOUNG MAN! - I'LL SEND YOU A DREAD!"

Calvin stopped as suddenly as a stalling car. He dropped the matches. He shook in a sweating sickness of terror.
"No," he wailed, in a tiny voice. "Oh, no... Not THAT... I can't stand the sight of those ghastly things!"
What is it?" screeched Rinty.
"Where is it?" screeched Jam.
"Get the yop out of there!" screeched Yopper.
Calvin turned and fled. He charged back towards the chorus of shrieking children. He bashed into the confused gang, causing them to tumble to the ground in a terrified heap.

"RUN! RUN! RUN!" hollered Rinty, as she led the escaping battalion back towards the bridge.

"DON'T GO! - STAY AND HELP ME!"

The leaves began to rustle and come to life as the bushes stretched out their thorny tentacles to stop the fleeing children... And then the dreads ALL switched on at the same time... Spiders, eclipses, and great gaping chasms of death.
Jam, Yopper, and Calvin all ran round in circles like a gang of headless chickens, bumping into each other, weeping and moaning, and ripping their clothes on the groping briars.
But this time Rinty stayed relatively cool and calm. She fought the dread that had leaped into her head... She could clearly see the bottomless pit of pain that went straight down to the Devil's doorstep... There was the slimy black hole

creeping closer to her, like the fire-belching split of a great earthquake... The rent in the ground reached her shoes, and she felt herself about to tumble down into the vision's dark depths -

"NO!" she screamed, slapping her own face until tears sprang from her tortured eyes. "IT'S A LIE! - THERE IS NO HOLE! - I DON'T BELIEVE IT!"

The hole vanished from Rinty's toes, the sun returned to Jam's dark world, and the spider stopped gnawing at Yopper's throat. Rinty's allies lay gasping on the ground. Their dreads had disappeared just as quickly as hers. Rinty had won her battle against the visions, but she still had to face up to the monster in the brambles who caused those fantastic fantasies. What other weapons did the Beast have in his armoury? She gritted her teeth, walking back towards the bushes. She shook from red hair to red trainers but she did it just the same - - And then she saw the magnificent monster -- The Beast Of Blackberry Lane! The terrible dread-maker was no longer than Rinty's forearm. It squirmed, slowly, from out of the hacked-away bushes, looking like a worn out snake. Rinty stared as the thing crawled closer to her toes...

"HELP ME, RINTY!"

The Beast was ALL body. No arms. No legs. The body was covered in sleek white fur. There was no head and there was no tail. There weren't even any eyes to tell which was front and which was back. The Beast reminded Rinty of a skinny draught excluder with most of the stuffing taken out...

"PLEASE HELP ME!"

Rinty watched, cautiously, as the pathetic creature edged nearer to her feet. Part of her spinning mind said: "Poor little thing!", while the more sensible part of her brain reminded her of the creature's awesome mental powers. She raised the hefty kukri knife above her head. She braced her legs to put all of her might into one powerful chop of destruction...

"PLEASE DON'T KILL ME!"

She had to kill the Beast - SHE HAD TO - This monster had brought a century

of terror to her village, and this might be her only chance to end the horror. It was up to her to destroy it. One, quick, slashing cut, and the nightmare would be over...

And then the Beast sent one, last, painful picture into Rinty's mind. The vision wasn't clear. It flickered and buzzed like a badly tuned-in telly... Rinty saw a wounded white fawn in a forest clearing. A young deer with an arrow protruding from its side. Frightened, alone, wanting its parents, and in terrible pain. The fawn was wailing for help, but Rinty was too angry and too full of hatred to understand that the picture was begging her to spare the Beast's life. As the fawn howled in agony, a strange, bright red fox stalked into the clearing. His eyes gleamed at the sight of the wounded white fawn - food that could not run away. The hungry fox licked his chops and approached the bleeding fawn with gleaming eyes and bared teeth...

Rinty swore, shaking the vision from her brain... She swung the two foot blade downwards towards the helpless Beast... The plea from the wounded white fawn went unheeded... The deer was about to be put out of its misery...

Just as Rinty's kukri began its descent of death, Inspector Braybrooke was making sure that all the audience was safely behind the red and white tape that twined around Old Baldy. By now the crowd had swelled by several hundred, with many outsiders having travelled to see the display. They were all giggling and sticking their fingers in their ears in pretend terror. Amongst this crowd, four pairs of parents were becoming rather puzzled and a tiny bit worried. It wasn't like Rinty, Jam, Calvin, and Yopper to miss such a spectacular free show.

''See,'' said Philbert Slick to his brother. ''I told you that if we demolished the field on a Saturday there would be thousands of spectators. It proves that WE have nothing to hide and it's a great advert for the company!''

''The crowd isn't far enough away,'' said Percival. ''You told that policeman that the charges were small ones and you've crammed in enough high explosive to blow up half of Essex. Those people at the front could get injured!''

''Accidents WILL happen,'' chuckled Philbert.

''Serves them right for being so nosy,'' laughed Percival.

The two brothers left the excited crowd and sneaked away to a far corner of the field where they sheltered behind a massive Essex Chemichem truck that was supplying the electrical power for the work. They watched as the firing box was switched on and the system prepared for the blasting.

"Would you care to do the honours, mister Clugg?" smiled Philbert, offering the computerised handset to the farmer. "After all, it is your property that's going to get a shake-up. Only right that you should be the one to pull the trigger!"

"Delighted!" beamed Clugg. "I love to see a good old bang! I was in the Royal Artillery, you know? I'll press that red button, right enough! It's almost worth losing a crop of wheat for, this is!"

"TEN MINUTES TO BLASTING!" boomed Inspector Braybrooke, over the loudspeaker... "CLEAR THE FIRING AREA! - TEN MINUTES!!"

CHAPTER SEVEN

THE BEAST'S STORY

An iron fist grabbed Rinty's wrist and stopped the death slice of the glistening kukri in mid-slice... The fist was no vision... The mighty hand was flesh and blood, and so was the huge body to which the arm belonged.

"Don't kill eee funny old creature," said Bobbee Lock, releasing his grip on Rinty's arm. "Eee old thing's only a little Squidler. Eee won't hurt eee, Wrint. Eee just wants to go home. Eee only wants his mum!"

Rinty was rage-shaking with anger and surprise.

"I've got to kill it, Bobbee," she snarled. "Don't you understand, dimbo? It's a monster... It's THE BEAST!"

"I understand a lot more than you think," whispered Bobbee. "Eee ain't no Beast, Wrint. Eee stop acting crazy and listen to the pictures in eee old red head! - Eee ALL look at the pictures!"

Yopper, Jam, Cal, and Rinty calmed slightly at the sound of the soothing words, returning slowly from their nightmare of shock. They began to use their brains again. They started to think. One by one they began to see the faint flickering message that the Beast was trying so hard to send to them... They saw the white wounded fawn with the cruel arrow biting into its young flesh. They saw - and at last they understood...

The Beast was represented by the fawn - He was lost and in great pain - He wanted to go home.

Teardrops blurred Rinty's eyes as the hatred drained away. She felt weak, exhausted, and rather ashamed... Rinty dropped the deadly kukri. The other kids lay down their weapons, sitting with Bobbee on the long grass. The strange, white furry animal lay before them on the dry brown carpet of crushed bushes. For at least a minute they stared at it in silence.

"I'm sorry that I called you a dimbo, Bobbee," sniffed Rinty, in a sad small voice.

"Dimbo eee self, old Wrint," grinned Bobbee.

"Yes," nodded Rinty. "I am - but I don't - I don't understand."

Then Rinty reached out towards the motionless Beast. She pushed both her hands beneath its skinny body and, very carefully, picked it up on her shivering fingers. The Beast didn't seem to mind being handled. In fact, it made a sort of rumbly sound that was similar to a cat's purr. Rinty laid the creature on her lap, stroking the sleek white fur. The silky coat lay flat and close, making the Beast look like a wet white otter. The Beast gave a wriggle of pleasure. Rinty could feel the ripple of starving bones beneath her gentle fingers.

"Eee ain't no soppy, pussy lap-cat," said Bobbee, but he said it with a sunlight smile on his handsome face.

"Ask him what he is?" whispered Jam.

"Ask him where he comes from?" hushed Calvin.

"Ask him why he's here?" hissed Yopper.

"Don't crowd him. You'll scare him and he'll send us more dreads," said Rinty.

As each person spoke, the Beast turned one end of his body towards them as if he were listening to every word of the conversation. In his own weird way, he was...

Eventually, he curled up on Rinty's lap and snuggled into an exhausted furry ball.

He told a story to the children and Bobbee, while appearing to be sound asleep. It wasn't the sort of tale that is made from words. It was built from millions of moving pictures and feelings. It flashed like a silent movie across the cinema screen of the blackberry bushes.

The children, and Bobbee, watched the vision in amazement. They couldn't understand it all but, when they told this story later to the host of press and television reporters, this was the message that they all agreed that the pictures from the Beast must mean:

THE BEAST'S STORY

Millions of years ago my ancestors walked on the surface of this planet in much the same way as you do - Then came the meat eaters. They chased our people and killed us. They slaughtered us by the thousand. Our little legs were useless and there was only one direction in which we could escape. We did the same thing as moles and rabbits but we did it more desperately. We burrowed into the earth. We came back to the surface at night to eat, then slid back into our burrows when the meat eaters returned with the dawn. But still our race was getting caught and being devoured. The meat eaters tunnelled after us and our tiny legs could barely dig quickly enough. Deeper and deeper we dug while our people grew fewer. We could no longer return to the surface and had to find nourishment by eating the soil itself. We learned to suck oxygen from the rocks in much the same way as a fish breathes in water. Many starved but some survived to run from the meat eaters who refused to give up. We grew fewer and fewer. When only fifty of our race were left, the meat eaters had us trapped against the impassable rock… We were about to become extinct…

Our great leader spoke to the feeble survivors. He insisted that we only had one chance of survival. We must use our special powers. The power that let us see into other creatures' minds. To talk without words. We must try to use the power in a way that had never been tried before. Perhaps it could be done if the whole tribe thought as one. We pictured a great swirling wind that could spin us though the earth and carry us to freedom to a land that was so deep that even the blood dripping jaws of our enemies could not reach us…

The people closed their eyes and imagined the swirl of rock-crushing power. Every brain worked together until we neared madness. It began slowly at first. A ripple of movement through the bodies of the tribe. Then it built into a whirlwind of motion which thrashed them around in the earth - through the rock and stone without even a scratch. Faster and faster. Deeper and deeper. Safer and safer… My people escaped!

The first "Swirling" had freed us from the jaws of death, but my race was deeper than any creature had ever been. Many more died but enough survived long enough to scrabble out a maze of tunnels and chambers. To grow in numbers and live in peace.

Millions of years of evolution saw our useless legs disappear, our unneeded eyes close, with only our warm fur to remind us of our past life on the surface. We have no language, for the pictures can say more than a billion words. The great force of the Swirling is only used once a year. Our Chieftain leads the ceremony in which we move a few metres through the earth, just to keep in practice in case the meat eaters return.

"You're telepathetic!" gasped Jam.

"Telepathic, nit!" corrected Cal.

"Tele-what?" puzzled Yopper.

"But why didn't you send the horrible meat eaters a dread to scare them away?" asked Rinty. "And if you live miles below the ground, what are you doing here?"

The Beast must have understood the rush of questions for he immediately answered with a fresh flow of pictures:

We did not send the meat eaters a dread because we did not realise that we had the power to do it until my grandfather made his famous journey to the surface and found that he had this great gift which he could use to protect himself. Travelling to the surface had always been unthinkable, but my grandfather had a burning desire to find out if the old legends were true. He built a secret tunnel by eating his way upwards. The task took him half of his life but, at last, he reached a layer of soft white rock just beneath the surface. From just above him he could hear strange rumblings and banging. He knew that he must be nearing the land of his ancestors.

One night, when all was still, he crawled out onto the white surface. He found that he was able to wriggle across the chalk, now that there was no pressure to cramp his movements. He sucked in the air which was so rich in oxygen that he felt giddy. When morning came he felt the heat of the sun on his fur. He felt wonderful. He felt free. He lay in the warmth of the legendary sun and was very happy.

Suddenly, the noise came rumbling back. He could sense the presence of other creatures although he could not see them. He did not know if these were the dreaded meat eaters, but he thought that he must protect himself in the only way that he could. He looked into the human minds and read the thing that each one was most afraid of, sending a vision of that horror into their minds. My grandfather had discovered the power of the dreads, as the humans ran screaming. My grandfather squirmed back into the burrow and ate out another tunnel to a place which he hoped would be safer. He gnawed to the surface in the middle of a blackberry forest. As no one ever entered the jungle of spikes, he knew that he was safe to explore from this base. He could not actually see this new world, but he could look into other creature's minds and see through their eyes. He learned about animals and humans alike. If ever he was trapped by a fox or a cat he would send them a dread and be left in peace as they yelped away. There were some problems for the great explorer. Even if he kept his nose buried in the earth it still hurt him to breathe the rich oxygen of your world. Also, the soil near the surface had been sucked dry of nourishment by the plants and he was gradually growing weaker. He was feeling old and feeble. He decided to return home before he perished.

He had just spent several days watching the children in the village. It was his way of saying goodbye. When he headed for his burrow in the brambles, he found that he was cut off from the entrance by noisy machines and gangs of workmen who were building a vast pile of earth between himself and safety. He tried to wriggle around the mound but he was much too weak. He tried to burrow through the mountain of soil, but the effort made him gasp and choke. He panicked, crossing the open space, heading towards a large gap in the wall of earth. He had to get under the unfinished bridge or die. A workman saw him and kicked him with a studded boot. He sent a nightmare dread into the human's brain, and the human ran off cursing and screaming. Another man hit him with a shovel and received a terrible vision of hell for his cruelty. There were so many humans that he could not fight them all. What was he to do? My grandfather could keep his journey to the surface a secret from the tribe no longer. He sent out a message for help.
Deep below the earth our leader heard the cry of despair. He hastily summoned

the whole tribe and called for a joining of the minds. He ordered another great Swirling. Thousands of our people spun through the solid ground. Up and up they spiralled. They whirled out into the air, whisked away my exhausted grandfather, saving his life... He never left the safety of home again.

"See?" said Jam. "That was when the railway workmen were building the bridge. They refused to work any more. I told you so!"
Rinty, Yopper, and Calvin nodded.
"Funny old story," said Bobbee.
"But it still doesn't explain why YOU are here," said Yopper.

The Beast sent out yet more pictures into the sky:
My grandfather was on his deathbed when he told me of his amazing journey and his rescue by the Swirling. I couldn't get the old chap's story out of my mind. One day I could stand it no longer. I left my parents sleeping and searched for my grandfather's tunnel. I found it in exactly the place that he had said. I wriggled upwards, stopping only to nibble a pathway through the parts of the tunnel that had crumbled and collapsed.

Finally, I reached the surface and felt dizzy in the air. There was no noise of machines or human workers in the chalk pit. It was overgrown with grass and brambles. No men ever came near me and most of the animals were harmless. Once a small fox tried to gobble me for supper but I remembered the things that my granddad had taught me and sent it a dread of a hundred foxhunters, complete with a pack of howling hounds, which soon made it shriek away in panic.

Later I wanted to see the place where you humans live. The second tunnel to the blackberry bushes must have been destroyed as the old chalk pit was enlarged, for I could not find it. I managed to wriggle up the steep sides of the crumbling pit and found the sheltering bushes by crawling along the surface. I slithered beneath the bridge and studied the villagers. The scene was exactly as my grandfather had described it. I became gradually braver. I sat and watched the humans work and play. The men who had built the bridge seemed to have gone, and I soon realised that no large human or animal could reach my shelter in the brambles. I soon discovered that I was growing weaker just as my granddad had warned. I was becoming rather feeble but I did not want

to return so soon. Then something awful happened to me...

I was watching a tall, handsome boy who was sitting on a log by the edge of the green. I was looking through the boy's own eyes at the work that he performed with ingenious hands. He was carving a chunk of wood into the shape of a beautiful butterfly. I had never seen anyone with such great skill. I was so intent on the magic craftwork that I failed to sense another human who was much nearer to me. Too late I saw the man. His head was full of swearwords and his hands were full of a twelve bore shotgun...

"Farmer Clugg, I bet a year's yops," Yopper guessed correctly.

...I sent a dread flying into the farmer's mind, but I was much too slow to react. His gun had already fired. Most of the blast hit the wall of the bridge, but several lead pellets dug deeply into my side. The farmer dropped his gun and fled from the power of the dread that I forced into his head. Why did he hate me enough to fire at me, without even checking to see what sort of creature I was? I meant the man no harm...

"He's an old loony," huffed Jam. "He'd shoot his own toes off if his new boots didn't fit him properly!"

...The farmer was gone, but now the tall boy was running towards me. I was about to fill his head with a dread, but in his mind I found only pity and kindness. The boy picked me up and dug the pellets out with his sharp knife. He washed my wounded fur then hid me beneath the blackberry bushes for safety. He came back every day to clean and comfort me. That unusual boy saved my life. He nursed me, and I slowly healed. He was very kind but rather odd. He had a funny name for me. He called me a - a Squidler. I never did find out what that word meant -

"Squidlers is Squidlers," grinned Bobbee.

"IT WAS BOBBEE!" yelled Rinty. "Don't you see? - That strange boy was Bobbee Lock! - Bobbee saved the Beast!"

"Well, I'll be yopped," gasped Yopper.

"I understand it ALL now," said Rinty. "The Beast sends EVERY adult a dread when they approach the bridge because he doesn't trust grown ups. He lets us kids through because he thinks that we might help him - just as Bobbee did. He only sends US a vision when we panic and run away. The dreads were

never meant to harm us. They were trying to make us stay. He's asking us for help like the white wounded fawn in the picture!''

''But he doesn't need our help now, because Bobbee cured him when he got shot - See? - There aren't any bullet holes in his fur coat,'' said Calvin.

''That was ages ago, when Bobbee was a kid!'' said Jam. ''Something must have happened to keep him here all these years!''

''Listen to eee old pictures!'' Bobbee insisted, as another display lit up the wall of the bridge.

One day, when my wounds were healed, I tried to wriggle back to my tunnel in the old chalk pit. I was already weak before the gunshot had nearly killed me, and it took me ages to make it back to the edge of the pit. When I finally arrived I was horrified to see truck after truck pouring rubbish into the pit. Fires were blazing night and day. The whole place stank of gunge, dead fish, horse manure, and smouldering rags. Worst of all, those Council refuse trucks were slowly burying my route back home.

Months passed before the fires went out and the rubbish cooled. The in-fill was covered by a layer of top soil and the old chalk pit had become a brown flat field. Eventually, that gun-slinging farmer came and planted corn. The wheat grew tall and thick, and at last I was left in peace to attempt to reach my buried tunnel. As soon as I tasted the soil I knew that something was terribly wrong. It wasn't just that the earth was full of garbage. There was something deadly in it... I found myself spitting out mouthfuls of poison... I slithered back into the brambles and waited for death to come -

''You mustn't just give up and die,'' said Rinty.

''Eee ought to get home. Eee mummy will be very cross with eee!'' said Bobbee.

''Don't be so stubborn and stupid,'' snapped Jam. ''You must tell your leader where you are, so that he can rescue you with the - Swirling - thingy!''

- I already have. The whole tribe has attempted to save me several times. The problem is that they cannot reach me in the bushes. You see, when they are swirling, nothing can harm them but, for the split second that is needed to gather me into the spinning crowd, they must become flesh and blood. For that second they are at the mercy of whatever element they find themselves in. If they appear in the brambles they will be spun into shreds. If they appear in the chalk pit's poison they will sizzle and fry. The only safe place for them to Swirl is in the wheat field beyond the dead corn. But that isn't near enough, for I haven't got the strength to reach them. They will Swirl for as long as their minds can stand the strain. They scream for me to come to the wheat field, but I cannot, so they have to give up and return home -

The children looked very sad and sorry for the Beast. All their fear and loathing had gone. They stroked his silky fur and felt the bones that had virtually no flesh on them... All their brains clicked into action at once.
"That's no problem," they chorused. "We'll save you! - We'll carry you into the wheat field! We'll do it right now!"
"You must hurry," sighed the pictures from the happy Beast. "The Swirling has begun already. My people will appear in the wheat field in exactly five of your minutes!"
Jam tipped the useless weapons from out of her school bag and laid the Beast delicately in its comfy bottom.
"We'll have to run right round by the village and up the track to the field. I can't do THAT in only five minutes," groaned Jam.
"Come on, you blob. We CAN do it!" cried the others.
The children were just sprinting through the bridge when they heard the clear voice of Inspector Braybrooke come floating across the blackberry forest. He was warning the crowd gathered round the field that the controlled explosions would begin in -

"FIVE MINUTES! - BLASTING IN FIVE MINUTES!!"

"OH, NO!" gasped the five running Beast-savers, as it suddenly dawned on their frantic brains that the whole Beast nation was about to Swirl into the centre of a gigantic explosion.

Farmer Clugg pulled his peaked cap down over his eyes to shield them from the sun, clapped his massive red hands together with glee and moved the firing box out from behind the Chemichem truck so that he could get a better view of his detonating field when he pressed the button. He was having a fantastic time!

Inspector Braybrooke was a slightly worried man. Explosions were not to be taken lightly and made the experienced policeman rather nervous. Were the hundreds of spectators REALLY standing at a safe distance? And, if the charges were only small ones, why were Philbert Slick and his gang of big bang experts sheltering behind that towering truck way across the field? It was all very worrying. And just look at that daft old farmer behaving like a toddler who has just been given a box of giant fireworks. Why on earth had Slick entrusted that twit with the firing box? The fool was walking nearer to the danger zone all the time.

"Mister Clugg," boomed the Inspector over his portable loudhailer, "I think that you should back-off a bit - just in case! - Better safe than sorry!"

"Mind your own business!" roared the rude farmer. "It's MY blasted field and I'll blasted well blow it up from any blasted place I please!"

"There won't be much of that old fool left when your charges explode," worried Percival, not really wanting a charge of murder to be added to his many crimes.

"Won't be much left of those simpletons in the crowd, either," smiled Philbert. "Still, serves them right for being so nosy. They look like the same sort of ghouls who drive miles to ogle the wreckage of a plane crash. They deserve to be blown to bits! - They came to see an exciting free show and they're going to get one - smack in the eyeballs! - I hope they enjoy it!"

"Just how much high explosive have you packed into this field?" whispered Percival.

"Enough, plus quite a bit extra!" chortled Philbert, his hideous laugh echoing across the silent waiting crowd and the silent waiting field that was going to erupt in:-

"FOUR MINUTES TO BLASTING! - FOUR MINUTES!"

CHAPTER EIGHT

CLUGG'S DREAD

The four children pelted across the green and took off down the road. Bobbee was already falling behind. His bulging body was built more for weightlifting than for sprint-speeding. They clattered past the empty houses whose occupants were all on the wheat field. Jam was puffing and panting.

"Give the bag to me," gasped Rinty, as they flew through the gate and onto the start of the dusty farm track that led to Old Baldy.

Jam threw the school bag like a rugby player and Rinty grabbed it skilfully, speeding onwards while leaving Jam and Bobbee to chug along behind. The sun's blaze beat down cruelly as the sweat flowed along their aching legs and the sun baked air burned their gasping lungs.

"This running - will - start up your asthma," choked Calvin. "Give - the - bag - to - me!"

"No - I'm OK." puffed Rinty. "I'll run into the field - You - tell the police - to stop the - blasting!"

Somewhere behind the crowd of people that encircled Old Baldy a loudspeaker cried out:

"THREE MINUTES TO BLASTING! - THREE MINUTES!"

Suddenly, the huge semicircle of spectators that was ten people deep in some places was split open, as a tall, gel-blond teenager pushed the public to one side and high-jumped over the ring of red and white tapes. Inspector Braybrooke glared at the wild-eyed figure, with his filthy T-shirt stuck to his

chest with gallons of sweaty glue, red scratches up both arms, and dozens of nondesigner rips in his faded blue Levi's. The blond youngster grabbed the Inspector by his shirt sleeve, pulled, twisted, tugged, and gulped out these breathless words:

"STOP! - GOTTA STOP! - BEAST SAID POISON IN THE FIELD! - ALL OVER THE PLACE! - ALL BE KILLED! - HIS PEOPLE ARE COMING! - THE SWIRLING!!"

"Clear off, my lad," snapped the Inspector, pushing the scruffy boy, who ponged of petrol and perspiration, back towards the safety zone.

"You - gasp - don't understand!" cried Cal, in frustration, as two young constables led him away.

Calvin was correct, the policemen did NOT understand. Before the lad had been hauled away a few metres, a second figure crawled beneath the ribbon and dashed up to the puzzled copper. This red-haired apparition, carrying two large canvas bags, seemed even less able to speak than its captured blond friend...

"PUFF! - OH! - SWIRLING! - GASP! - DANGER! - PLEASE! - OH, PLEEEEZE!"

While Rinty choked for words and air, a third child ran up to him. Smaller, darker, even filthier, and waving a long leather strap in the policeman's face. This kid was so out of breath that he only managed to splutter something that sounded strangely like: "OH! - Y-O-P!"

Inspector Braybrooke had the awful feeling that his tidy, orderly world was going into a manic spin.

"TWO MINUTES TO - ER - BLAST OFF!" shouted farmer Clugg, pointing delightedly at the face of the digital clock on the top of the firing box.

Then the crazily wheezing red-head groped around in one of her bags, pulled out a Ventolin asthma inhaler together with a Gurkha knife, swore, threw the pack down, rummaged around in her other pack and lifted out what appeared to be either a white cuddly toy or a white weasel with its legs and tail chopped off...

"SEEEE?" shrieked Rinty.

The Inspector did not "SEEEE!" at all.

Rinty waved the Beast under the policeman's nose...

"SHOW HIM, BEAST! - SHOW HIM!" she wailed.

An instant picture filled the policeman's brain. In a few seconds he was forced to SEEEE the truth... Empty, overgrown chalk pits being filled in with Council rubbish and smouldering night and day - Being filled in with building site rubble - Being filled with clean fresh top soil - Being filled (IN THE MIDDLE OF THE NIGHT BY MEN WEARING PROTECTIVE RUBBER SUITS AND GAS MASKS) with gallons of poisonous chemical waste - Waste that was pouring through black hosepipes set deep into the fresh top soil - Hosepipes that were connected to a massive tanker truck that carried a very familiar logo - The same logo that was painted on the lorry in the distance - The badge of Essex Chemichem (The Ozone Friendly Company).

The vision switched off, leaving the policeman's jaw sagging with shock.

"ONE MINUTE TO THE BIGGEST BANG YOU'VE EVER SEEN!" screamed farmer Clugg.

Now Inspector Braybrooke could SEEEE it ALL...

He saw and he understood...

He grabbed his megaphone:

"STOP THE FIRING! - CLEAR THE FIELD! - ARREST THE SLICK BROTHERS! - DETAIN THOSE CHEMICAL WORKERS! - CLUGG, PUT DOWN THAT DETONATOR! - THIS LAND IS FULL OF POISON!!"

The orders crackled out across the silent land. The orders were so loud that they could have been heard in Cambridge. Policemen rushed to obey. Percival and Philbert Slick rushed towards Percy's waiting black Porsche. Some of the crowd grew jittery, began to feel uneasy, and shuffled away. Only farmer Clugg did not hear a single word. He was a man in a deadly trance. He stared with red rimmed eyes at the digital screen of the firing box as the red numbers - those fascinating numbers - ticked from:

50 to 49 to 48 to 47 SECONDS!

He didn't even hear the howl of the black Porsche's tyres as they chewed up the cornfield and struggled to get a grip on the dry dust-dirt. The sports car missed the farmer by millimetres as the Slick brothers made a frantic rush to escape from the sounds of "poison? - Poison? - POISON!!" that shrieked from the confused crowd. Percival slammed the car into a higher gear while a shower of stony debris shot out like bullets from the whirring wheels. Percy jumped on the accelerator, spinning the skidding car in the direction of the track. The twin horns honked a warning at the line of puzzled people in the Porsche's path... Fifty spectators and three policeman dashed to the right... Fifty spectators and five policeman dived to the left... The Porsche had only to slice through the plastic ribbon like some supercharged athlete at the end of a one hundred metres race, for the two Slick brothers to have been long gone and free as two wicked birds... There was only one small thing that blocked their path to freedom...

The "small thing" was a dark haired, curly nine-year-old. His face was streaked with sweat, his teeth were clenched tight, and held firmly in his fist was a long leather strap that was whirring around his determined young head. "Put your foot down," yelled Philbert. "Squash the grubby vermin into hedgehog stew!"
The long leather slingshot spun faster and faster.
"Whooo! - Whooo! - WHOOO!" sang the whirling thong as it slashed through the heavy air.
The Porsche roared straight towards the tiny figure, with its horns howling...
The figure refused to move.
"WHOOO! - WHOOOO! - WHOOOOSH!" Yopper let fly with his sharpest stone.
"WHEEE!" the Porsche thundered towards him.
"SMASH!" exploded the tinted windscreen... The large chunk of Essex flint sailed in between the Slick brothers, chipping a nick out of Philbert's left ear, and chanked its violent way out of the rear window.
"I can't see a blasted thing!" wailed Percival, as the windshield turned into a blinding spider's web of busted glass. Philbert hauled on the steering wheel while the two rogues fought to gain control of the cavorting sports car.

Yopper rolled to one side as the Porsche came burning through the red and white ribbon. The racer revved off the track, bumped and bucked over the cornfield like a horse with a thistle under its tail, and slithered straight towards

the tangle of blackberry bushes. The powerful motor forced a ragged path into the brambles for about thirty metres until the groping jungle of prickles dragged it down onto its metal knees. It roared, coughed, chugged a cloud of black fumes, and died. Philbert punched Percival in the ear and informed him that he hadn't got enough sense to drive a pram. Percival called Philbert an ''obnoxious, germ-licking, overdressed tonk-head!'' They threw the two doors open and attempted to make a run for it... They did not get very far. They hung in the tangle of needle tipped brambles, with their arms outstretched and scratched to tatters, looking like soggy, red stained washing on a spiky clothes line. It was going to take a very long time to release them from their spiky handcuffs and snap their wrists into metal ones.

20 to 19 to 18 to 17 SECONDS!
Farmer Clugg was still hypnotised by the power that he was about to unleash. ''Grab that lunatic before he presses the button!'' yelled Inspector Braybrooke.

15 to 14 to 13 to 12 SECONDS!
Seven policemen raced towards the crazy farmer with his itchy finger on the blasting trigger.

9 to 8 to 7 to 6 SECONDS!
Not one of those seven racing policemen could possibly cover the distance in time.

''SEND HIM A DREAD!'' hollered Rinty, pointing the furry Beast in the direction of the barmy farmer...

A vision clicked on instantly in Clugg's pulverised brain... The same vision that the farmer had been hammered with many years before, after he had shot the weird, white, fluffy ''snake'' thing down by the bridge in Blackberry Lane... The same ghastly vision that turned his sleep into scream-dreams at least once a week... A dog... Oh, no!.. Not simply a ''dog'' - A snarling, black, fire-eyed hound out of hell - The dreadful dog with the foaming fangs that dripped with disgusting disease - A dog that charged at him from the far side of Old Baldy - A dog that leaped in slow motion bounds - A dog whose howling yellow teeth were heading straight for his leathery red neck - A mad dog whose body was burning with rabies and whose jaws were aching to munch

and scrunch at his bones -
4 to 3 to 2 to 1 SECOND!
The red numbers flickered their message on the firing box in the shaking farmer's fingers -
FIRE! - FIRE! - FIRE! -
The red light flashed the angry word while the red button yearned to be pressed.
"Come on, you blasted monster," hissed farmer Clugg, as the nightmare hellhound bounded towards him with splashes of sickly foam splattering its charging chest. "You don't scare ME! - I'm gonna blast you up into Saturn's rings!"

When Clugg had first seen the devil-dog vision in Blackberry Lane, he had dropped his smoking shotgun and run away from the white Beast that he had wanted to pump more death pellets into. When he suffered the weekly nightmare he would wake trembling in a bath of cold sweat and lay shivering until the cockerel crowed - but not any more - "OH, NO, MY BEAUTY! - COME YOU ON IF YOU DARE! - I'VE HAD ENOUGH OF THIS DAMN DREAD! - I'M BUYING YOU A ONE WAY TICKET TO HELL!"
The farmer waited for his monstrous mongrel to reach the explosive charges then he would punch the signalling "FIRE!" button and send that evil brute to meet its maker in tiny, black furred pieces of blood and bone.

CHAPTER NINE

THE SWIRLING

And then the hot air shimmered and shook... The corn began to flap and flail as the dusty soil was sucked up into the clear blue sky... The Swirling was coming. The dust twirled into a massive blurred spiral of whirring sky. The wind wailed, causing the wheat to collapse in a circle as large as a football pitch... The Swirling yowled and howled like a blast from the devil's trumpet. A mighty corkscrew of tiny particles formed in the middle of Old Baldy right above the high explosive welcome that was about to be unleashed.

The remaining spectators shrieked and fled for their lives.
The Essex Chemichem workers ran side by side with the panicked policemen. Faster and faster spun the ice-cold whirlwind from the depths of the earth. Faster and faster ran the crowd of people.

Everyone ran, except for Bobbee, Calvin, Jam, and Yopper, who were shaking with tremors of terror but at least had some vague knowledge of what was causing the gale of stinging grit.

All except the Slick brothers who hadn't a clue what was happening and had both fainted from shock.

All except Rinty who chewed her lip until she tasted blood but still had guts enough to walk forward to the freezing edge of the Swirling's cyclone...

All except farmer Clugg, whose dread had long been switched off by the Beast

in Rinty's arms, but whose crazy mind was still only capable of watching and waiting for the black, rabid hound to reach the minefield of high explosives. And then the Swirling changed.
The whirlwind was suddenly packed with millions of spinning white streaks... The Beast's nation had arrived to save their long-lost brother.

"Goodbye, Beast!" whispered Rinty, as she cuddled the warm white fur to her freckles and buried her nose in the silky softness of her new friend's coat.

The Beast was unable to "speak" a farewell to the child who was saving his life while risking her own, so he sent a picture into Rinty's mind that she would always remember: There was the wounded white fawn, as before, bleating with pain and horror at the sight of his bright eyed enemy. There was the hungry fox, licking his chops and moving in for the kill. Suddenly the fox darted forward - Instead of fastening his jaws around the jugular in the fawn's neck, he clamped his gleaming fangs onto the deadly arrow and yanked it out with a swift snap of his head. He licked the wound clean and, magically, the skin began to mend, until the bloody hole closed and was completely healed - The white fawn jumped for joy, scampering off into the safety of the forest. -

Rinty held the Beast out at arm's length into the edge of the speckled, white Swirling. Her hands shook in the icy whirlwind's blast...
"Come back one day!" she sniffed. "I'm sorry that I didn't understand you. I'm sorry that I hated you. Please come back to see us again. Things will be better next time!"

She watched as the vision of the forest glade blazed once more to give her a last message then faded away... She smiled... The Beast flicked out of her hands like a small wisp of thistledown grabbed in the force of a hurricane. His white body was instantly lost amongst the millions of others who all looked exactly the same... The Swirling was gone... The Beast, and his rescuers, were safe... All that remained to mark the spot where the amazing flow of energy had volcanoed forth was another neat circle of flattened corn.
The field was silent once more - well - almost silent -

"-Just a bit closer, my old beauty!" whispered a mad malicious farmer.

"EEE OLD FOOL'S GONNA DO IT!" yelled Bobbee, pushing and hurrying the four bemused children from the centre of the wheat field...

"Come you on! - Just a few more feet, you puppy full of puke!!"

Bobbee hurled the kids forward towards the protection of the Essex Chemichem truck but they were still several metres from safety when -
" - almost! - ALMOST! - N-O-W!!!"
Farmer Clugg punched the red "FIRE!" button.

The whole field erupted as forty massive power-packs of high explosive sent forty columns of whistling rubble high into the darkened, rumbling sky...
A churning black cloud hung over the field... Hundreds of spectators stopped running, twirled around, and stared with their eyeballs out on stalks.
The thunder died slowly away until the only sound to be heard was the faint chink of tiny chiplets of flint as they floated back to the shattered earth...
A tall figure staggered out of the filthy smog of smoke... The giant carried a small, curly-haired boy on his muscular shoulders and, trailing behind him, clutched in his mighty fist, a straggly line of three more children. All hand in hand, only barely able to hobble along, and black as chimney sweeps who have just worked a double shift... All were completely safe and, more or less, sound. The crowd blinked in wonder through the mist, mumbled, rubbed their stinging eyes, cheered, then rushed back towards the heroic band of battered Beast-lovers.

It was several more minutes before Inspector Braybrooke put on breathing apparatus and went back into the thinning smoke. He found a once proud Porsche car covered in dents and slashes with most of its paint peeled off and its tyres ablaze. He found the two Slick brothers with their expensive clothes in tatters and their hair completely sizzled off. Percival was crying for his mum, while Philbert was gibbering like a manic monkey and singing: "Goodness Gracious, Great Balls of Fire!!" He found the Essex Chemichem truck with its windows shattered and a melted logo badge which now read: "SEX ICHEM - THE ONE FRIEND COMPANY" He also found a completely naked farmer still clutching the firing box and still rambling on about a rabid black dog that was coming to get him.

By this time Rinty and her mates were being led away home by happy parents and grateful neighbours.

Rinty noticed that her chest was getting tight and groped in the back pocket of her multicoloured shorts where she usually kept her precious inhaler. The pocket was empty.

"I've left my puffer in the bag on the field," she gasped, feeling the panic of losing her medicine making the wheezes worse.

"Calm down, love," smiled Rinty's mum. "There's another one at home"

"You don't need that stupid inhaler," snorted Calvin. "You've just run a mile flat out, been buried in a cloud of dust - AND - HORRORS! - cuddled a FURRY, FLUFFY, ALLERGENIC creature right by your nose - FOR AGES - AND it had no effect on you at all until you began to worry about losing your puffer - Your asthma is ALL IN THE MIND!"

"Rubbish!" wheezed Rinty. "It's ALL in my LUNGS!"

"Talking of things in our minds," said Jam. "You never did tell us what YOUR dread was, Calvin - What horrid vision did you see in the blackberry bushes when you tried to set fire to them?"

"I didn't get a dread," snapped Calvin. "My mind was too powerful for the Beast to enter! - I concentrated the force away!"

"Cobblers!" grinned Jam.

"Well, if you didn't get a yopping dread, what were you screaming and yelling about? asked Yopper.

"I - er - I - If you must know - I saw something that I can't stand - It wasn't a dread. I saw it for real in the bushes," spluttered Cal, his face growing red as a raspberry pie beneath its coating of soot.

"What was it then?" persisted the gang.

"Nothing! - Shut up about it!" gruffed Cal.

"I know what eee saw! - I do! I do!" laughed Bobbee. "Eee saw a little, old whiskery-worm - That's what eee saw!"

"Ha - Ha - Ha!" bellowed Jam. "Bobbee means a hairy caterpillar! A great, big, teenage, cool dude like you is scared of itchy-twitchy, hairy-scary caterpillars - WHEE-HEE!!"

"Shut your rattle, you grease-bodied, walking doughnut!" snarled Calvin, grabbing

Jam by the scruff of her dust-coated blouse.

"Now, now, now!" soothed Rinty. "Calm yourself, Calvin dear! - Remember - IT'S ALL IN THE MIND!"

Calvin bunched a fist and aimed for Rinty's cheeky chin - but - then he began to giggle - soon everyone was laughing.

Two months later several hundreds of reporters clamoured around the Courtroom steps to hear the sentence passed on the now notorious Slick brothers. Both Percival and Philbert were given twenty years in prison and were ordered to pay a massive fine to cover the cost of cleaning up Old Baldy and all the other Essex chalk pits that they had dumped their poisonous waste in.

Farmer Clugg was neither fit to be charged nor able to plant next year's crop in his newly cleaned soil. To this day he sits in a locked room with padded walls, a disconnected firing box clutched in his hairy hands, staring into space as he waits to get another chance at blowing his dreaded, black rabid dog off the face of the planet as it makes yet another charge at him... He mumbles the same threats over and over: "I'M READY FOR YOU, BLAST YOUR GIBLETS! - COME YOU ON, MY BEAUTY!"

Bobbee took down his "DANJER!" sign. He had originally carved it when the Beast was shot by farmer Clugg. He never meant that the sign should protect the people from a dangerous "Squidler". It was intended to keep nosy folk away from the injured Beast that he was trying so hard to cure. He recarved the sign and put it back. Now it simply says: "Blackberry Lane" and includes a picturesque scene of a wonderful white windmill. Of course, there are no windmills in Cutters Bend, but Bobbee likes them, and for Bobbee that is reason enough for putting one on the glorious picture.

Jam and Rinty are still best friends. Yopper usually plays with kids his own age, and Calvin has gone back to strutting around with his teenage gang, but none of them will ever forget the day when they went out to face the dreaded dread-machine.

At first, the children told the true story of their adventure to the host of notepads, cassette recorders, and video cameras that seemed to follow them everywhere. After a short while they began to leave the Beast out of the saga,

as it became obvious that no one believed a word that they were saying. Now they only talk, rather modestly, of the day when their heroics saved hundreds of people from the sinister plans of the fiendish Slick explosion. Soon the country forgot all about the incident at Cutters Bend and moved on to other world-crunching news.

Rinty never forgot about the Beast. She often walks along Blackberry Lane, under the peaceful bridge, and into the wilderness of brambles and thorns. The berries have rotted and the leaves have fluttered to the ground. Perhaps next summer the villagers will gain confidence and return to pick the free fruit spectacular - or perhaps they'll remember their dreads and go shopping at Tesco instead. Rinty likes to make sure that the Beast hasn't returned to Cutters Bend. She doesn't want to miss her friend, because she is confident that one day it will return... She recalls the end of the Beast's last vision as he spun from her fingers into the heart of the Swirling mass, the part that she keeps a close secret, even from her friends - the most important part:

As the newly healed, white fawn trotted off into the safety of the forest, he stopped, turned, and waited for the fox to follow him... The fox dashed after his new friend, and they scampered off to play in a place where it doesn't matter what kind of creature you are... Rinty knows that the white fawn represents the Beast and, in her mind, it's pretty obvious who the cheeky fox is - Isn't the fox's hair long, straggly, and shimmering red? - Isn't his face flecked with cornflake freckles? - Doesn't he appear to be wearing a pair of multicoloured shorts - and - what on earth is that funny bulge on his bottom in the place where a back pocket might be? - Could it be the L-shaped bump of a Ventolin asthma inhaler?

Oh, yes! ...... One day the Beast WILL return!

CHAPTER TEN

SAYONARA

The British Airways jet levelled out high above the Essex marshes. Stansted Airport was already fifty miles behind. The Japanese student opened her terrified eyes and stared, wildly, all around her... The plane wasn't on fire and the pilot was still at the controls. She let out an enormous sigh of relief. She suddenly realised that she was clasping the hand of the old gentleman sitting next to her. She was squeezing so tightly that the ancient soldier's fingers had turned white. She let go, apologised, and looked awfully embarrassed. The old gentleman smiled and told her that he was glad to be of service and added that, at his age, it was rather a novelty to have a pretty young lady hanging on to your hand. He also said, in a quiet calm voice, that it was no use being afraid that a disaster might happen. Your life was in the hands of the Gods, so why worry about it?

The student relaxed. She hadn't slept a wink in her comfortable bed at the Saffron Motel. The memory of the dread had kept her tossing and twisting all night. She thanked the old man, yawned, and fell asleep. She would not wake up until the plane had landed safely at Tokyo Airport. She would never be scared to fly again.

The old soldier also drifted off while thinking about the highlights of his wonderful holiday. He was very glad to have visited England at last. In the war his officers had told him that the English foe were monsters and he had believed them. He had really been convinced that the English ate Japanese prisoners for breakfast. Now he had seen the truth… People were people! English or Japanese - Most good, a few bad. The English were sometimes a tiny bit weird, but they certainly were not monsters… And those four children - the ones on the green in Cutters Bend - the place where the houses had grass on the rooftops - the kids with hatred in their hearts and death in their brains. He had a hopeful feeling that when they finally faced whatever awful Beast it was that they had been setting out to conquer they would come to the same conclusion that he had found… That the only beast that must be killed is the one that lives in your own frightened mind… For, although there was once an animal from an unexplored land, there never was a ''Beast'' in the brambles of Blackberry Lane.